JASON ZEITLER

The Breatharian

Stories

Polyphony Press | Tucson, AZ 85719

The Breatharian and Other Stories

Polyphony Press
Tucson, AZ 85719

These stories are works of fiction. The names, characters, and incidents portrayed in them are the work of the author's imagination. Any resemblance to actual persons, living or dead, events, or localities is entirely coincidental.

Some of the stories in this collection have appeared elsewhere, in a slightly different form: "A Trick of Light" in the May 2017 issue of *SandScript*; "The Water's Edge" in the June 2017 issue of *Out of Print*; "Remembrance" in the Winter 2018 issue of *Midwestern Gothic*; *Like Flesh to the Scalpel* in Running Wild Press's 2018 novella anthology; "Inglorious Carnage" in Running Wild Press's 2019 short-story anthology; "A Familial Duty" in the April 2023 issue of *Spellbinder*; and "The Breatharian" in *Two Thirds North*'s 2024 anthology

Manufactured in the United States of America
Library of Congress Control Number: 2023921054
ISBN: 979-8-9892692-0-4

For Darshini

Contents

The Water's Edge

I WASN'T AT MY SISTER-IN-LAW'S in Sri Lanka at the time her dog Siri died, but the peculiar circumstances of his passing, from a Westerner's perspective anyway, have haunted me ever since. Probably it is *because* I didn't see the event firsthand that it made such an indelible mark on my psyche. In telling Siri's story, my hope is to once and for all exorcise from my mind the unsettling images of his death, images that might otherwise linger in my memory indefinitely.

To be honest, I am surprised at myself for being so affected by the death of a dog. I have never really been very fond of dogs as a species. They drool too much. They stink. Many of them have a kind of permanent halitosis. And if they haven't been well trained or trained at all, they are nothing short of a nuisance: pawing you, jumping onto you, sniffing you in places you would rather not be sniffed. I remember the last dog I had as a child. He was a chocolate cocker spaniel named Alex, and to describe him as boisterous would be a gross understatement. Like most dogs, he didn't like being left at home alone. Whenever my family would leave the house, even for a short time, we would return to his staccato woof-woof as we pulled into the driveway. He would hardly let us open the front door. The moment we forced our way in he would welcome each of us in turn by jumping at our midsections.

Then he would launch into his ritual circuit around the house, sprinting from one room to the next, scaling the living room furniture and other incidentals along the way. It was exhausting just watching him. My parents probably should have had him trained, but they didn't have the money or the time. In hindsight, I feel ambivalence toward Alex. I miss his undying affection, just not the ways in which that affection usually manifested itself.

So it is all the more strange that I grew to love Siri. My guess is that it had something to do with his being a Labrador. Big working dogs, especially hunting dogs like the Labrador, are more tolerable than small, yipping ones. I once went pheasant hunting with my father in South Dakota on a ranch that used black Labs as trackers on guided hunts. They were majestic animals, their muscles rippling and their coats glistening as they methodically worked their way through the fields of corn, happily flushing birds for us to shoot.

Shortly before Siri's death, my wife Rajivi and I arrived in Colombo for our annual summer holiday in Sri Lanka. On our itinerary was a trip to the dry zone in the southeast of the island, a weekend at Arugam Bay and a few days at my sister-in-law's bungalow near Tissamaharama. Whenever we are in Sri Lanka, a stay at Sonali's place is always a welcome respite from the diesel exhaust and garbage-ridden streets of Colombo. Her bungalow, which is adjacent to Yala National Park where she works as a field biologist for the Sri Lankan government, sits on a two-acre strip of land overlooking a small lake, or tank. The tank attracts wildlife from all over the area, including elephants from the park. We sometimes sit for hours on Sonali's veranda training our binoculars on the scrub jungle just south of the tank. If we are lucky, we see an entire herd of elephants from calves to matriarch steal from the jungle, make their way cautiously to the water's edge, and then drink and play and bathe with an air of contentment not even a Buddhist monk could attain.

On the day of our road trip to Tissamaharama, we arrived late in the afternoon. It was hot, over 90 degrees Fahrenheit, and a strong wind was blowing in off the Indian Ocean. At the gate to Sonali's property, Gnanasiri, the old caretaker, greeted us. He was a funny-looking little man. The few teeth he had left were stained purplish-brown from chewing betel. He usually wore only a sarong so that his paunch, supported by his otherwise fit five-and-a-half-foot frame, was bared to the world. Gnanasiri's teeth and belly notwithstanding, he was an excellent caretaker, and his cooking abilities alone made him a prized employee. Even now, as I pulled our vehicle into Sonali's yard and parked beneath the immense canopy of a fully grown mango tree, I could smell the thick gravy of Gnanasiri's pork curry.

Gnanasiri took our bags, and we settled into the guestroom. Since Sonali failed to appear, we assumed she was in Tissamaharama buying groceries for our visit. However, Gnanasiri informed us that she had been out searching for one of her two dogs since early morning. Apparently Siri went missing the day before while Sonali was away on a camping trip upcountry. The signs weren't auspicious, Gnanasiri explained, as the dog hadn't been seen by anyone for over twenty-four hours. Also, something had spooked Tunza, Sonali's German shepherd; he had been hiding under the picnic table on the veranda for approximately the duration of Siri's absence and had refused to come out even when tempted with his favorite food, Purina dog chow mixed with wild-boar curry. Gnanasiri speculated that Tunza had seen a *yakka*, an evil tree spirit, and that only a realignment of the stars would now bring him out from beneath the picnic table.

"And what about Sonali?" Rajivi asked, a concerned look

on her face.

She would be back before sunset, he said, in time to join us for dinner.

Sonali did not return for dinner. Rajivi and I waited at the picnic table until our meal of pork curry, lentils, and roti grew cold. Not that the cold food mattered, for we had long since lost our appetites, the Siri affair having cast a pall over our trip. We sat at the table for a while in silence and picked at our food with our fingers. The sun had already set, and the geckos were gathering about the electric lanterns, feeding on mosquitoes and other insects and making their incessant squawking sounds. Every now and then Tunza shifted his position at our feet. Gnanasiri, I thought, was right about one thing: the signs so far were not good. It occurred to me, and I suspected to Rajivi as well, that the longer it took Sonali to return, the less likely it was that Siri would ever be found.

Our experiences with Siri had been limited to our holidays in Tissamaharama, but nevertheless we developed a deep connection with him. He was the runt of the litter and so was only two-thirds the size of the average juvenile Labrador. Yet he had that unmistakable muscular build unique to his breed. He loved the water and at heart, if not in practice, was a retriever. I remember how at the word "ball," he would bolt from Sonali's bungalow and run a circuit from one end of the yard to the other until someone threw the ball. At times like this, Siri reminded me of my childhood dog Alex, except that Siri somehow seemed more dignified.

I reached across the picnic table and touched Rajivi's hand. She looked up from her plate and said, "Sad, no?" The question was rhetorical, of course, but I answered it in the affirmative anyway.

Not until well after dinner did Sonali finally return home. She came in looking haggard, her clothes covered in dust. Her search for Siri had been unsuccessful, and now she feared the worst. Earlier that day Janaka, one of the park rangers, noticed a crocodile circling a spot in the tank, about twenty feet from shore. It could mean only one thing, Sonali said. The crocodile was guarding a kill, which it had lodged in the lakebed. Sonali and Janaka decided, now that the search for Siri on land had been exhausted, to turn to the water. Rajivi remonstrated, pointing out the obvious dangers of such an endeavor, but Sonali was adamant. At first light tomorrow, she and Janaka would search the tank.

I lay in bed that night thinking with dread about the possibility that a crocodile had taken Siri. Perhaps it was a temporary lapse in my imagination, but I couldn't think of a worse way of dying. One of those African antelope documentaries I had seen recently kept coming to mind. In it, the wildebeests are on their annual migration from the Serengeti to the Masai Mara. In the river-crossing scene, the camera pans in on a fifteen-foot Nile crocodile half-submerged in the shallows of the Mara River, waiting for its next victim. No sooner has the first of the wildebeest leapt into the river than the crocodile strikes. It clamps onto a leg and attempts to pull the wildebeest under. The wildebeest struggles to free itself. In an instant several other crocodiles swarm, collectively making the kill in a frenzied twisting of bodies until the wildebeest is torn limb from limb or drowned or both.

I fell asleep hoping a similar fate hadn't befallen Siri.

The next morning I awoke to the noisy sound of a koel, an Asian cuckoo whose onomatopoetic call makes the loud meow of the peacock seem muted by comparison. I groped my way through the opening in the mosquito net and, straining my eyes in the dim light, checked the time. It was half past five. Rajivi had already gotten out of bed.

I found her and Sonali standing on the veranda, drinking tea and looking out toward the tank. They appeared to be deep in thought, so much so that I hesitated to disturb them. As I approached, both of them smiled, with their eyes as well as their mouths. Without speaking, Rajivi made a slight movement of her head in the direction of the tank, of the surrounding fields, of the beautiful sprawling jungle that was Yala. I followed her line of vision. To the southwest, a lone farmer stood in the middle of a vast paddy field. He was dressed entirely in white and had a wide-brimmed straw hat in his hand. Above him in the sky, a half-moon hovered. In the opposite direction, to the east, the horizon glowed pinkish-orange. And due south was the tank, a morning mist rising off of it. On the other side of the tank where the jungle began, I could just make out through the mist a peacock perched on the topmost branch of a ranavara shrub.

"I should be getting ready," Sonali said, breaking the silence. She reached through the iron grill separating the veranda from the house and set her teacup onto the kitchen counter. "Janaka will be here soon."

"And there's *nothing* we can do to change your mind?" Rajivi asked.

"No," she said, "there isn't."

Later that morning, at Rajivi's suggestion, I offered to act as lookout for Sonali and Janaka while they searched the tank. Janaka helped me climb the nearest palu tree, where I positioned myself with the binoculars at the best vantage point. Word must have gotten around about the morning's search because ten or twelve of the neighbors turned up. They came in twos and threes, talking excitedly and pointing at Sonali and Janaka as they prepared to enter the water. When they noticed me in the tree, they became demure, then amused. I was suddenly more interesting to them than what they originally came to see. They giggled and whispered, every now and then one of them looking at me furtively: the ridiculous *suddha*, the white man, in a tree, decidedly out of his element.

Before I could remove the lens caps and focus my binoculars, Sonali and Janaka were in the water. They waded in slowly. Their pace was clearly making Rajivi nervous; she kept motioning to them to hurry back to shore. The water was up to their chests by the time they reached the spot the crocodile was circling the day before. With the binoculars, I scanned the tank for any signs of danger.

Together Sonali and Janaka searched the lakebed with their feet, moving in tight concentric circles. Sonali stopped, as if she had found something, took a deep breath, and disappeared beneath the water. Meanwhile I thought I saw what looked like a crocodile's eyes and snout drifting about thirty yards from shore. I shouted a warning to Janaka. In his shrill voice, he shouted back in acknowledgement, and then he, too, disappeared beneath the water. The crocodile, or what I thought was a crocodile, was now no longer in sight. Either it had submerged, in which case there was still danger, or it had swum away, scared off by the noises we were making.

A few seconds later Janaka and Sonali emerged from the water, a black mass in their arms. They hurried back to shore. Once there, with a kind of reverence, they placed their burden onto the ground. I took a closer look with the binoculars. The black mass was Siri's remains. His body, after two days in the water, was badly decomposed. In places his coat was shorn to the flesh, presumably the handiwork of fish. He had extensive puncture and slash wounds on his stomach and hindquarters. One of his legs was missing. I lowered the binoculars; I had seen enough.

It was then I realized what had driven Tunza to hide beneath the picnic table: he witnessed Siri's death. I imagined that something—a herd of water buffalo, say—had disturbed the dogs as they dozed on Sonali's veranda. Growling and barking, they jumped up, raced to the back gate, and somehow slipped unscathed through a narrow gap in the barbwire. At the approach of the dogs, the buffalo dispersed, leaving an open pathway to the tank. The temptation was too great for Siri. He leapt into the water without hesitation, swimming as if in the act of retrieval. Tunza meanwhile only waded in, shin deep. An instinctive sense of danger, perhaps some atavistic remnant of the wolf, prevented him from going farther. He stood there watching Siri, his ears erect, his tail curved upward. The water stirred near Siri and a violent commotion erupted. Tunza let out a single guttural bark, which sounded like a warning, or a protest. Whatever the bark was meant to be, it came too late. Where Siri had gone under, the water rippled for a moment and then darkened a blood red.

From my perch in the palu tree, I had the urge to rage against crocodiles, to voice what Tunza could not. It struck me that crocodiles and their kind were nothing but brutal killing machines. What redeeming qualities did they have? I could think of none. They were cold-blooded in every sense of the word, and they preyed indiscriminately on both the weak and the strong. Siri was proof of that. A crocodile had taken him not because he was weak or unfit but because he had the misfortune of not being jungle-wise, and of being in the wrong place at the wrong time.

The cacophonous, laugh-like call of a peacock in the distance brought my reverie to an end. I glanced down through the branches. The neighbors huddled around Siri's remains as Rajivi and Sonali unraveled a saffron-colored blanket that looked vaguely like a monk's robes. I hung the binoculars around my neck and began to descend. Halfway down, I lost my footing. Only a well-placed lower branch kept me from crashing in spectacular fashion to the ground. I righted myself among the branches, more embarrassed at my clumsiness than hurt. As I did so, I heard several voices say "Sad, no" one after the other in a torrential outpouring of sympathy. And in that moment, squatting there in the tree like an oversized macaque, I imagined that those solicitous words were intended for me as well as Siri.

A Familial Duty

I DIDN'T WANT TO SEE HIM, but I had no choice. His name was Ranil, and he was a second cousin of my amma's. While I was visiting Amma and Thatha at their place in Colombo, on vacation from my job in Boston over the summer, I made the mistake of mentioning I would be passing through London on my way back home. I had plans to stay at an apartment near Paddington Station for a couple of days and to visit some old friends from my time at Oxford. As soon as Amma heard about it, though, she said, "Oh, *putā*, you have to see Ranil while you're there. He would so appreciate a visit from you. He's all alone, you know." That was her way, to make me feel guilty. So much for my plans, I thought. I knew the moment our conversation ended, Amma would be on the phone with Uncle Ranil to tell him the "good news" of my visit to London, and it would be a major faux pas for me not to go see him after that.

There was a reason Uncle Ranil was "all alone," as Amma said—or rather, several reasons. In his late sixties by then, the man was a sort of caricature: flabby; a disheveled, bushy head of hair; and a voice so squeaky and high-pitched it made your ears hurt. And he had become utterly strange in his old age— to call him eccentric wouldn't have done him justice. Because of Uncle Ranil's behavior, his wife had long since divorced him, and now even his children avoided him. I remember staying with him once while I was still at Oxford, some ten years ago. His wife had just left him then, and already he was letting himself go. His bachelor pad, a flat in Wembley, was a disaster area. I am a fastidious person, and so I could hardly believe what I was seeing while I was there. It looked like he hadn't cleaned the flat in weeks: papers and books strewn everywhere, urine-encrusted toilet seats in the bathrooms, unmade beds in the bedrooms. The worst part was the kitchen. There were unwashed dishes precariously stacked three feet high in the sink and bits of food on the floor and the countertops. There was even evidence of a fire above the stove, the wall and surrounding cupboards black with soot. Also, he was a hoarder and liked to buy things in bulk—a Costco dream. On one side of the island in his kitchen stood a large plastic bin the size of a beer keg. Out of curiosity one day, I opened it while he was out grocery shopping and found it brimming with ketchup packets. A lifetime supply of ketchup packets! And that was back then. I dreaded to think what his flat looked like now, ten years on.

And then there was the story my little sister Manjula told me. Last year, Uncle Ranil went to Sri Lanka for a few weeks. He didn't have immediate family of his own to stay with, and paying for a hotel was out of the question, so he invited himself to Amma and Thatha's in Colombo. They couldn't very well refuse him: it wasn't the South Asian way. When Uncle Ranil arrived at the house, he came crashing in with three enormous Delsey suitcases, giving the servants orders as if he owned the place. He seemed to be drunk, probably from the bottle of whiskey he bought at the airport duty free to give to Amma and Thatha for their hospitality. Manjula was so angry with him afterward, she decided to get back at him by ransacking his suitcases the next day while he was out. She never imagined what she would find. One suitcase contained several dozen tins of sardines and a second one nothing but cans of pork and beans. The third suitcase was more intriguing. It contained clothing along with various odds and ends, including boxes of chocolates and bags of hard candies. Digging more deeply, she unearthed a large package of condoms and almost screamed when she realized what they were. *Eww,* she thought, *what was he planning? Wasn't he too old for that?* Then she saw the women's panties. She picked them up and held them before her. They were hot pink with little embroidered hearts on them and so large Manjula could have worn them as a nightshirt. *A gift for some woman he knew in Colombo?* Manjula was laughing hysterically when she later told me about all this over the phone.

As expected while I was still in Colombo, Amma contacted Uncle Ranil the moment she and I finished our conversation about my trip to London, and arrangements were made. I offered to meet him on Great Russell Street in front of the British Museum the morning after my arrival at Heathrow. At the time, the museum had an exhibit on Indigenous Australians that looked interesting, and I thought that if my time with my university friends was going to be cut short because of Uncle Ranil, I might as well get something educational out of it.

Uncle Ranil got to the museum before I did. A block away, I saw him standing there on the pavement, looking a little dazed, in his white oxford shirt and black pants, his belly sticking out like a pregnant woman's. He didn't see me until I was almost on top of him. He squinted, gave me an uncertain wave, and came forward to greet me. Hardly had he done so when he tripped on a crack in the pavement and fell into a nearby group of tourists.

I probably ought to have mentioned earlier that in addition to his other issues, Uncle Ranil was almost blind. What he needed was a seeing-eye dog or one of those Hoover canes to get around with, but he refused to use either because he was in complete denial of his problem. I was mystified as to how he had even gotten to the museum that day, given his poor eyesight.

I reached him as a couple of the tourists were helping him to his feet. "So sorry," he was saying in his squeaky voice. "I don't know what happened. My apologies."

"Uncle Ranil, are you all right?" I asked, grasping his hand.

He had a faraway look in his eyes and seemed not to recognize me. Finally he said, "Haresh, my boy, how are you?" and I noticed his pants were covered in dirt, and a button on his shirt was unbuttoned, exposing his navel.

"I'm fine," I said. "It's you I'm worried about. Are you sure you're all right?"

He made a half-hearted attempt to brush the dirt from his pants. "Don't worry about me, my boy. Everything's hunky-dory, as they say."

"I'm glad to hear it." I had intended to hug him, but now on closer examination, I decided against it. He must have recently dyed his hair because it was pitch black, and dye was running down the sides of his face and onto his shirt. He also had done something to his eyebrows, shaved them perhaps and then penciled in new ones. He looked like a clown, or a 1930s Hollywood actress.

"Let me look at you," he said, squinting at me sideways, as I tentatively put my arm in his and led him up the steps of the museum. I thought it an odd expression for someone who could barely see two feet in front of his face. Still squinting at me, he squeezed my arm and said, "You've become a man, by God. All that time on your own across the pond has done you good."

"It's kind of you to say so, Uncle Ranil." At the same time I was thinking, A stab in the dark? Who wouldn't mature in ten years' time?

In the museum, I suggested we do the Australia exhibit on the upper level first and then the Egypt exhibit on the lower level after that, time permitting. I headed for the elevator bank to the upper level, but Uncle Ranil called me back. He wanted to use the stairs, he said. Made entirely of marble, the staircase was an exhibit in itself, and he wasn't about to use the lazy man's way out and lose the chance to get some exercise, of which he wasn't getting nearly enough these days. I had no desire to argue, so I gave in and took him up the stairs. I assumed that if he used the railing and I helped him a little, everything would be fine. I ought to have known better.

As we inched our way up the stairs—Uncle Ranil huffing and puffing at every step, with me at his side—he began telling me about a recent trip to Italy he went on with some friends. A week into the trip his passport was stolen by a pickpocket, or so he said. The way he told the story sounded so much like a confession, I suspected he was giving me only half the truth. He was so careless and near-sighted, he probably had misplaced the passport and now was too embarrassed to admit the fact. I was thinking as much—we were about a third of the way up the staircase now—when he suddenly stopped talking, squinted up the stairs with a frightened expression on his face, let go of the railing, and turned around and started descending the stairs. Except that it wasn't descending so much as hurtling two steps at a time. I tried to lunge for him, but it was too late. A second later his feet went out from under him, and I watched in horror as he pitched forward and slid head first down the stairs like a human toboggan, until finally he crumpled into a heap on the nearest landing.

As all this played out, an elderly British couple stood at the bottom of the stairs, looking on. I heard the husband say, "Good grief," and saw him rush up the stairs at the same time that I was rushing down.

"Uncle Ranil," was all I said when I got to him. I didn't kneel down. Somehow I couldn't bring myself to be sympathetic. I kept thinking that what had happened was my fault, and I resented him for it. Not to mention my trip to the museum was ruined.

"Is he all right?" the British man asked as he approached us on the landing. "My wife has gone for help."

Uncle Ranil made a high-pitched whining noise, rolled over onto his back, and stared blankly at the ceiling.

I didn't say anything. I just looked at his funny mop of hair, thinking, What's Amma going to say? She'll never forgive me.

"That's a good sign," the British man said. "I mean that he's able to move."

A paramedic from the museum arrived, along with the elderly British man's wife. The paramedic knelt down next to Uncle Ranil and took his pulse. As he did so, he looked at me and asked, "What happened?"

"He lost his footing and fell down the stairs," the British man chimed in before I could answer. "It was the craziest thing I've ever seen."

Uncle Ranil appeared to come out of his torpor, and the paramedic asked him a series of questions. What's your name? What day is it? Who's the current prime minister? Uncle Ranil answered all the questions with flying colors. Surprisingly, he even managed to answer the question about how many fingers the paramedic was holding up. "He seems to be all right," the paramedic concluded as he flashed a penlight into Uncle Ranil's eyes. "But I recommend he get some rest." He asked me if I was a relative.

Reluctantly I said I was.

"Maybe you should take him home," he said, putting the penlight back into his pocket.

"I'll do that," I said. But I had no intention of taking Uncle Ranil home. I just wanted to be rid of him, to put the whole ridiculous affair behind me. I would, I told myself, take him to the closest Tube station from the museum, Tottenham Court Road. And I would worry about smoothing things over with Amma later.

We all helped Uncle Ranil to his feet, and I thanked the paramedic and the British couple for their help.

"We don't have to go, you know," Uncle Ranil said to me as the others left. He insisted he was perfectly fine. "It was nothing—a bit of a tumble was all."

"I think it's best if we go," I said, taking him by the arm and leading him down the stairs.

The entire time we walked to the Tube, by fits and starts as Uncle Ranil tripped over one crack after another in the pavement, he kept telling me how good he felt—"Never felt better, in fact"—and how he and I could always turn back to the museum if I wanted. Trying not to sound curt, I told him repeatedly that I didn't want to, that it would be better if we simply called it a day.

We got to the station just as a train was pulling up. I helped him over the gap between the platform and the train, through the car doors, and onto a seat. The instant we said our goodbyes, I made for the doors. I shouldn't have, but I felt a sense of relief as I stepped out of the car. When I turned around to watch the train depart, I started to lift my hand to wave but immediately stopped myself. Uncle Ranil looked so alone sitting there, with tears in his eyes, I thought that if I were to wave to him, it would only add insult to injury.

The Breatharian

THE RUMOR GOING AROUND THE VILLAGE was that the holy man had survived for weeks on nothing but air. It was said that in all that time he had not once stirred from his spot on the outskirts of the village, where he sat lotus style beneath a palu tree. Crowds had begun to gather to catch a glimpse of him. One day Sumith and his friend Bandula were walking home from school, wearing their white uniforms and black backpacks, when they encountered the crowd. They, too, had heard the rumor—many, many times, in fact—so they knew why the people were there.

At the back of the crowd Bandula stood on his tiptoes, straining to see what the spectacle was all about. Despite a recent growth spurt, he was short for a fourteen-year-old and a bit on the chubby side. "Shall we go see for ourselves?" he suggested, again rising onto his tiptoes in a vain attempt to get a better look.

Sumith grunted to communicate his displeasure at the suggestion. He was a year older than Bandula, and it seemed to him that his seniority obliged him to be more restrained. Besides, he was not overly curious when it came to spectacle. He derided people who stopped to gawk at traffic accidents, for instance.

Bandula pretended not to have heard Sumith's grunt. "Can you believe he hasn't eaten or drunk a thing for forty days and forty nights?"

"Don't lie," Sumith said.

"No, man," Bandula protested, "it's true." His belly quivered as he laughed. "Ask Lalitha."

Just the mention of Lalitha, Bandula's older sister, made Sumith blush. The other day he had been bathing in the local tank with his family and a number of other villagers, including Lalitha, when her water cloth came undone, exposing one of her breasts. She was only seventeen, but already she looked like a woman of the Sigiriya frescoes. Sumith had turned away, as if he had seen nothing, but the vision remained seared in his memory.

Bandula was still laughing. "Lalitha saw him herself last evening. She says that even if he does eat, it can't be much because he's an absolute beanpole."

Sumith's resistance, like the holy man's body, was wearing thin. Ascetics always piqued his interest. He enjoyed learning about the Buddha and often read Jataka stories and other religious texts. He looked at Bandula, said "Are you coming, then?" and pushed his way through the crowd.

The holy man was even thinner than Lalitha said. He wore only a sarong so that his protruding ribs were visible, and his skin was taut and leathery like the headcover of a Kandyan drum. He might have passed as one of the twists in the palu tree's trunk. Was it really possible, Sumith wondered, that the man had not eaten for weeks? He had that strange, otherworldly look of a saint. He also had scraggly, shoulder-length hair and a bushy, chest-length beard similar to the madman who had appeared in the village a few years ago claiming to be Jesus. Sumith knew very little about Jesus, but he knew enough to know that he was not South Asian and that he did not have green eyes. And surely—Sumith laughed inwardly at the thought—Jesus did not have brown skin, as he was not a Cochin Jew.

"They say he's what's called a breatharian," Bandula said quietly and reverently as he and Sumith stood there gawking at the front of the crowd.

The breatharian sat motionless in the lotus position with his eyes closed and an utterly serene look on his face.

Throughout the rest of the day Sumith's thoughts returned to the breatharian. Where did he come from? Why did he choose Sumith's village? And what exactly was a breatharian, anyway?

That evening at dinner, Sumith spoke to his family just enough not to arouse their suspicions that his mind was elsewhere. He ate quickly, excused himself, and went to his room.

He lay in bed reading the *Dhammapada* by the light of an oil lamp, but he could not focus. Eventually he gave up. Something was not right, he thought, about the breatharian's going weeks without food or water. In biology class recently, he had learned about the digestive system, and he recalled Ms. Kusuma saying that the average human could not survive more than three days without water.

But even supposing it were true that the breatharian had fasted for weeks, what was the point of it? To show off? If so, that would not be a very Buddhist thing to do. The Buddha himself rejected extreme asceticism, believing that such practices only added to suffering and did nothing to bring about enlightenment.

Sumith sat up in bed and removed his shirt. All the mental exertion had caused him to sweat. He glanced toward the open window. It was a sultry, moonlit night. With each passing moment, the singing of the tree frogs out in the garden seemed to grow louder.

There was no getting around it: he would have to speak to the breatharian. His mother would not be happy about that, but he had a right to think for himself. She often told him he could pursue whatever religious or intellectual inquiries he chose, in the spirit of the Buddha's teachings. He remembered a couple of lines from a poem she used to read to him, "On Children": "You may give them your love but not your thoughts, / For they have their own thoughts."

Just then his mother appeared in the doorway of his room, looking concerned. She had yet to change out of her sari and into her nightclothes. "Is something the matter, darling? You weren't yourself earlier."

He did not want to lie, so he said nothing.

She came over and untucked the mosquito net from under the mattress and sat down on the bed beside him. "Does it have to do with a girl?"

"Aiyo, no," he said, suppressing a laugh. "Well, at least not in the way you're thinking." He had yet to tell someone about Lalitha's water cloth.

"What do you mean?"

He told her then, and they both had a good laugh.

As time passed, the crowds on the outskirts of the village grew smaller and smaller until eventually no one turned up to see the breatharian at all. Only Sumith's interest did not wane. He told Bandula of his plan, and each day after school for a week, the two of them did dry runs to see if the breatharian was still in the same spot. Sure enough, each time the boys crossed the bund, with the tank on one side and the rice fields on the other, they would see the breatharian in the middle distance, as motionless as a statue and as emaciated as ever.

On the seventh day, when they reached the end of the bund on their way home from school, Sumith said rather mysteriously, "It's time."

"You mean now?"

"Yes, now."

They stood with their thumbs in the straps of their backpacks and squinted in the late afternoon sun. Green bee-eaters flitted about here and there on the dirt road, dustbathing or eating insects caught on the wing. In the shallows of the tank a lapwing erupted into its loud, scolding *did-you-do-it* series of calls. A stray dog materialized out of nowhere, trotted up to the boys, and unceremoniously sniffed at their feet.

"Shoo," Bandula said and kicked at the dog.

It yipped and ran off.

A voice suddenly came from the opposite end of the bund. Lalitha was running toward them. "There you are, you idiot! I've been looking for you everywhere."

The boys exchanged glances.

Lalitha came up to them with her arms akimbo. She wore a floral chintz dress, and her hair was in plaits.

Sumith blushed and averted his eyes.

"What is it?" Bandula asked her with irritation in his voice.

"Mother needs your help. Father had to go to Tissa for supplies, and one of the cows is calving." Their parents were subsistence farmers.

Bandula gave Sumith an apologetic look. "Sorry, brother, I have to go."

"What are you doing here, anyway?" Lalitha asked scornfully. When neither of the boys responded, she glared at Sumith. "This was your idea, wasn't it? You're an even bigger idiot than he is." She looked in the direction of the breatharian.

"I should have known you wouldn't be able to keep away, being a religious zealot yourself."

"Sumith just wants to talk to him," Bandula blurted out.

Sumith frowned. That was what he got, he thought, for entrusting Bandula with a secret.

"Are you still here?" Lalitha shouted at Bandula. "Go on. Mother's waiting."

"Oh, all right," he said and trudged back across the bund.

Lalitha followed him. After a few steps, she said over her shoulder, "Looks like you're on your own now." Then with a flick of her plaits she hurried after Bandula.

Sumith watched them go. As they receded from view, a herd of water buffalo disturbed a crocodile sunbathing on the shore of the tank. It galloped to the water and dove in, scaring up a purple heron as well as egrets, ibises, lapwings. The heron emitted a croak-like groan as it lumbered into the air. In a body the birds scattered helter-skelter, flew out over the rice fields, circled back to the tank, and then landed in the water one by one.

Sumith turned around and made his way down the dirt road. With each step his heart beat faster. As he drew closer to the breatharian, he saw that his eyes were closed. He stopped a few paces away from the man and awkwardly waited for him to open his eyes. He considered saying something or clearing his throat, but he was afraid the breatharian's eyes might be closed for a good reason. What if he were meditating? Or what if he slept during the day because he stayed awake all night on the lookout for leopards and bears?

As he waited, it occurred to him why the breatharian had chosen this spot. It was a ruggedly beautiful edge of scrub jungle. Between the palu tree and the jungle was a stand of rosewood and Ceylon oak. A muster of peafowl, with their iridescent blue and green feathers, foraged in the undergrowth.

Cassia bushes and lantanas of various colors were in bloom.

The breatharian opened his eyes. "I have been expecting you."

Sumith's heart skipped. He looked back over his shoulder, as if the breatharian were speaking to someone else, but no one was there. "You've been expecting *me*?"

The breatharian waggled his head. "That surprises you?" He gestured toward the bund. "I saw you and your friend."

A brief silence ensued as Sumith contemplated the implication of the breatharian's remark. So, he had been watching Sumith and Bandula watch him? That meant that his eyes had not been perpetually closed. Sumith scrutinized his face. The man had the features of a Sinhalese, and he spoke fluent Sinhala, but he did not behave like a Buddhist at all. Sumith wanted to get straight to the point and ask what a breatharian was, but he was afraid it might make him sound like an idiot. Instead he asked haltingly, "Why are you here?"

The breatharian smiled and said, "With every breath we take, we inhale two things: air and prana." He turned his head and with a sweep of his arm indicated the jungle. "Both of these things are in abundance here."

Sumith knew the word "prana" from studying Hindu literature in school. It meant "life force." But what *that* meant he had no idea.

"Prana is the energy that connects and animates all things," the breatharian continued, seeming to sense Sumith's confusion.

So the breatharian was a Hindu. That would explain a lot. Maybe he was a yogi. Yogis sat in the lotus position and meditated just like Buddhists did. Sumith had no interest in becoming a yogi, but he was glad he had come. He felt as though he were in school receiving a lesson, and that suited him just fine.

With the backs of his hands resting on his knees, the breatharian positioned his fingers into the jnana mudra. "Prana exists everywhere. It is all around us. In stones and earth. In plants and animals. In you and me. Even in the air itself." He took a deep breath. "Can you feel it?"

Sumith admitted that he could not.

Suddenly the breatharian's face darkened. "Then you must learn!" he cried, and appeared to wince at his own words.

A peacock screamed in among the trees, and then peacocks all over the jungle joined in, making one guttural scream after the other.

Amid the din, the breatharian smiled a mad contorted smile and in a softer voice added, "You must learn to surrender your mind." Jerkily he thrust up a hand with the palm facing outward. He remained in this pose for nearly a minute. Then he returned his hands to his knees, re-positioned his fingers into the jnana mudra, and closed his eyes.

The lesson, it seemed, was over.

The moment Sumith set off for home he knew he would have to speak to the breatharian again. Now that the ice had been broken, it would be that much easier. Besides, Sumith was unsatisfied with the way the first meeting went.

A strong wind blew as he walked home. Dust collected in his eyes and nose and left a gritty film on his uniform. Once he was home, he bathed at the well and put on a clean T-shirt and a sarong. Then he fixed himself a plate of unripe mango covered in chili powder and went barefoot out onto the veranda. This was the life, he thought, as he sat down on a chair: enjoying the simple pleasures, impermanent though they were. The air smelled faintly of the sea. The trees—frangipani, mango, neem, tamarind, weera—were flowering or in fruit.

Purple bougainvillea and red hibiscus, which formed a border around the garden, were bursting with flowers.

Still, he felt unsettled. Something the breatharian said was bothering him: that bit about surrendering the mind. It was easy for someone the breatharian's age to advise the surrendering of the mind, since he already knew the way things were. But Sumith had yet to experience the life of an adult, not to mention the touch of a woman. How could he possibly surrender his mind without knowing what he was surrendering?

The raucous, two-note call of a koel pierced the air, rousing Sumith from his thoughts. He resumed eating and was on his fifth slice of mango when his eyes were drawn to the field opposite the road. Some of the neighborhood children were there flying kites, and a small boy was chasing an errant spool across the field. The boy squealed and, giving up the chase, looked helplessly up at the sky. A hundred feet above ground his kite whirled uncontrollably and then nosedived into the canopy of an enormous palu tree.

Sumith laughed to himself, looked out over the garden, and savored another slice of mango.

Early the next morning before school Sumith went to see the breatharian. This time his eyes were open. He waved to Sumith. "Hello, young man. How are you? Have you come to ask more questions?" Behind him the jungle teemed with birdsong.

Sumith nodded but suddenly felt shy. The man might take offense if Sumith were to ask him how he had survived so long without food and water.

The breatharian smiled with his eyes. "If you will not ask me a question, then I will ask you one. Did you know that prana provides nourishment for the body *and* the soul?"

"You believe in a soul?" Sumith said, overcoming his reticence, even though it was not the question he had intended to ask.

"And you do not?"

Sumith shook his head. He was surprised at the breatharian's ignorance. How could he be so disciplined in body but not in mind? It was common knowledge that no self-respecting orthodox Buddhist believed in a soul, or a permanent self. The concept did not jibe with the fact of the impermanence of all things. Sumith learned that at temple from an early age. And more recently, what was it that Ms. Kusuma said? That the universe itself was in constant flux, expanding inexorably toward infinity? So how could anything possibly be permanent? "I'm a Buddhist," Sumith said.

The breatharian smirked. "Even Buddhists need prana to survive."

Blood rushed to Sumith's face. Something was different about the breatharian—not just in his manner and in his voice but in his appearance, too. Sumith had the urge to flee. "I have to be to school." He quickly turned tail without breaking into a run, his heart pounding violently. He found himself on the other side of the bund before he knew it. Halfway to school he bumped into Bandula and Lalitha and almost wept with joy at the sight of them.

"Brother!" Bandula said, clapping Sumith on the shoulder.

Sumith clapped him back. "Glad to see you too."

Lalitha made a face and went on ahead.

Bandula stared at Sumith inquisitively. "So?" he said, unable to contain his curiosity. "How'd it go with you-know-who?"

Sumith described their first conversation but kept quiet on the second.

"Did you find out how he does it?" Bandula probed.

"There wasn't time for that."

Bandula shrugged. "Oh, well. Better luck next time."

They took each other by the hand and walked silently for a while. Lalitha was far ahead of them now. Other children in white uniforms dotted the road. Here and there along the way, adults stood in their yards, brushing their teeth or watching the children go by.

Bandula grinned from ear to ear. "Aren't you even going to guess how things went with the cow?"

"False labor?"

"No, man." Bandula laughed. "Just the opposite." He let go of Sumith's hand and held up two fingers. "Twins. Both bulls. Can you believe it? We had a devil of a time getting them out."

Sumith said nothing and was silent and thoughtful the rest of the journey to school.

The villagers spent the following day in religious observances for Vesak. In the evening people were out in full force. The men and boys wore white kurtas and sarongs, while the women and girls wore white saris or dresses. Colorful paper lanterns hung from trees along the roads and from eaves of buildings. Oil lamps flickered on windowsills and on altars. In front of the temple an electrically lit scene from a Jataka story was on display. All over the village food stalls offered free food and drinks.

It was customary on festival days for Sumith and his family to go to temple. They did so on this day like any other, and after they returned home, Sumith told his parents he was meeting Bandula at a food stall for ice cream. He left the house and sneaked unnoticed to his bedroom window and climbed through. Two minutes later he re-emerged—wearing a black long-sleeve shirt, denim jeans, and his backpack with the machete his mother used to crack coconuts—and headed for the road.

He looked out of place among all the people dressed in white. But no one paid any attention to him. On the outskirts of the village, instead of stopping at a food stall, he veered off toward the bund. He reached it just as the sun was setting. In the tank, water birds waded silently, getting in their last fishing before dusk. A solitary bull elephant stood nearby in a patch of rushes and reeds spraying itself with its trunk.

Sumith gazed across the bund. He could not see the breatharian, so it was safe to assume that the breatharian could not see him, either. He took out the machete, then stole down the embankment and made his way along a path that encircled the tank. Where the water ended, he stepped off the path onto a grassy field, avoiding elephant and buffalo dung as best he could in the crepuscular light. He skirted the jungle's edge for a few hundred meters until he reached the opening of an elephant trail, at which point he disappeared into the brush.

The full moon was already high in the eastern sky. Sumith followed the trail by its light. He was well into the jungle when he heard branches breaking. He crouched down behind a tree, his heart racing. Whatever the animal was, it sounded big. His worst fear was that it might be a sloth bear because they were so vicious.

Then he heard more branches breaking, and the unmistakable rumble of an elephant. He breathed a sigh of relief. Elephants he could handle, so long as he kept his distance. Their eyesight was poor. He squinted into the darkness. Thirty meters away was a solitary bull easily weighing over six tons. If Sumith had not heard it and known what to look for, he might never have seen it: its gray hide blended in perfectly with its surroundings. It stood there gently swaying its head and trunk from side to side, its tusks glimmering in the moonlight. Sumith remained still, until the elephant went crashing through the brush toward the festival lights, intent on raiding farmers' crops while everyone was preoccupied.

He continued on the trail, tightly gripping the machete. Shortly he reached the breatharian and hid behind a cassia bush and stood there, watching. The breatharian was still sitting beneath the palu tree. Peafowl roosted overhead; Sumith could hear them rustling in the branches of the trees. From somewhere far off came the *tu-whoo-hu* of a fish owl.

An hour went by, and the breatharian did not move. The man was determined, Sumith would give him that. But so was Sumith. And he was bent on finding out the truth. He would stay here all night if he had to, even at the risk of his parents' sending out a search party for him.

Another hour went by, and still nothing happened. Sumith's eyes grew heavy. He sat down to make himself more comfortable and within minutes dozed off.

He awoke to the sound of voices. He jumped to his feet and peered through the branches of the cassia bush. A figure was standing in front of the breatharian, arguing and gesticulating wildly. Sumith was too far away to see or hear clearly. He put away the machete and crawled through the dirt and creepers until he was seventy or eighty feet from the palu tree.

He lay motionless with his head slightly raised. He could see the figure clearly now. Every feature, protruding ribs and all, was identical to that of the breatharian. What was being said was still unintelligible, but it did not matter. Sumith's heart sank in spite of himself. A part of him did not want it to be true. Deep down, he wanted to believe in something beyond himself, something more vital and permanent. What if he simply chose now not to believe his eyes? But as he blinked in the moonlight, he knew with absolute certainty that he was seeing things as they truly were.

A Trick of Light

ALAN WAS EXPECTING THE REFRIGERATOR to arrive any moment now. With a slight grimace on his face, he peered through the front window of his house to check for the delivery truck. There was no sign of it. He wondered where the damned thing was. He had been given a delivery window of ten to noon, and, according to his watch, it was already 11:58. He could not understand why the delivery process was so imprecise. Seriously, how hard could it be? Delivering appliances was not exactly rocket science.

A minute passed. Again he looked out the window, his patience running thin. But still there was no truck, and he found this intolerable. It was bad enough, he thought, that the scheduling had been so free and easy. Now to top it all off, after two hours of waiting, the blasted delivery was late. And to think how he had gone out of his way, even canceling several of his patients' appointments, to be at home for the delivery. As he paced back and forth in the entryway of his house, looking at his watch for the umpteenth time, another grimace, like a nervous tic, formed on his face. He could not brook the fact that something as mundane as a refrigerator had interfered with the mental health of his patients. "Unbelievable," he muttered to himself as he went to the sideboard and picked up the phone. Violently with an index finger he punched in the dispatcher's number.

The truck, apparently, was on its way, or so the dispatcher assured him. But Alan was *not* assured. Instead, he became belligerent. The assurance was too little too late, he said. The truck should have been "on its way" two hours ago. Sarcastically he asked the dispatcher how a company could be run like that: there was about as much precision in scheduling a two-hour delivery window as there was in holding up a moist finger to gauge the direction of the wind. In the world of business, he continued, were not customers supposed to be sovereign? *He* was a customer, and he could say with certainty that he did not feel sovereign in the least. Before slamming down the phone, he added for dramatic effect, "Instead of serving me expeditiously, you've wasted my time. Don't you know I have work to do, things to get done, a life to lead?"

Just then the doorbell rang. In a huff Alan went to the door to answer it. On the veranda were two deliverymen: one tall and skinny, the other short and fat. Even without trilbies and black suits, the two men looked strikingly to Alan like Dan Aykroyd and John Belushi from the movie *The Blues Brothers*, and coincidentally displayed above the breast pockets of their uniforms were the names Dan and John, respectively. Behind them a brand new stainless steel refrigerator gleamed in the sunlight. Alan could hardly keep from laughing, despite his anger.

"Sorry we're late," the Belushi-lookalike said, a stupid, ingratiating grin on his face.

"It's quite all right," Alan said, holding back a smile. He always found it easier to be truculent over the phone, to berate a disembodied voice, than to do it in person. Besides, the appearance of the deliverymen and the hilarious coincidence of their names had temporarily suppressed his ire.

Together the two men, Dan and John, tipped the refrigerator

back onto the dolly and prepared to maneuver it into the house.

As Alan made way for them in the entryway, he was conscious of the fact that while he had been browbeating the dispatcher over the phone, the deliverymen must have been outside his house unloading the truck. It also occurred to him that if he had been patient enough to wait even thirty seconds more, he might have avoided the confrontation entirely. It was a disconcerting thought, one that caused an excess of blood to rush to his face. Stepping back into the shadows of the entryway to hide his embarrassment, he forgot to go through his usual spiel about being careful on using a dolly in the house. The next thing he heard was a grating sound of metal on wood as an edge of the refrigerator caught the doorframe. He winced and clenched his teeth but held his tongue.

For their part, the deliverymen went on as if nothing had happened. "The kitchen?" the two of them asked hurriedly in unison, apparently in an attempt to cover up their transgression.

That's right, Alan thought: *Ignore it, and it never happened.* Without a word, his lower lip quivering slightly, he pointed toward the hallway that led onto the kitchen.

"Thanks, man," Dan said, disregarding formalities. Then he and his associate briskly wheeled the refrigerator down the hallway to be unloaded.

Alan stayed back to investigate the damage to the front door. He knelt down near the doorframe. There was a gouge in it a half-centimeter deep, wood and paint curled up on one side like grated cheese. He reached out and lightly ran a finger along the splintered groove, as if disbelieving his eyes. The repair job, he figured, would take him a good fifteen minutes to complete. It would not be as simple as touching up paint; it would require using wood filler as well, along with the associated drying and sanding time. He was incensed at the thought. Yet more of his precious time would be wasted. One consolation, he told himself, was that he could feel justified again in having made such a fuss over the tardiness of the delivery truck. Although technically it had not been late, that no longer mattered. He had been right all along in thinking that the deliverymen were somehow derelict in their duties. He vowed that before the day was through, he would give the dispatcher another earful, whether or not that was the right person to whom to voice concerns about quality control.

The deliverymen had installed the refrigerator by the time Alan came into the kitchen to inspect their work. "What do you think?" John asked him, waving an arm in front of the new appliance like a game-show host presenting a prize.

"It looks fine," Alan said. As he spoke, he only half took in the refrigerator. He was too preoccupied with Dan—who at the moment was standing presumptuously on the other side of the room in front of the sliding-glass door and looking intently out onto the backyard—to devote his full attention to anything else.

"This is quite a place you've got here," Dan observed. He motioned in the general direction of the exterior wall surrounding the house and added, "I especially like what you've done with those roses."

Alan was annoyed with the man for lingering when he was not wanted, but he also felt a sense of pride at the compliment about the roses. He had spent a great deal of time during the past two months nurturing them. Now they were in full bloom, the vines covered with delicate white and yellow flowers. He himself would sometimes sit in the garden and do nothing but stare at the roses, and he could not begrudge the deliveryman the same pleasure. He was about to make some banal remark about the flowers' being on their last legs when a handheld computer was thrust into his face.

"Sign here, please," John said, tapping the signature line on the computer screen.

Alan signed with his finger.

"You're all set." John put a spread-eagled hand on the door of the refrigerator and began to rattle off a long list of GE-appliance amenities.

Alan cut him short. "I know all that," he said impatiently. "That's why I bought the refrigerator in the first place." He had no interest in small talk, not even about roses for which he had a passion and certainly not about refrigerators; he just wanted the two men gone before they did any more damage. "Now if you'll excuse me," he said. "I have work to get back to."

"Oh … yeah … sorry," John mumbled. "Well, anyway, I hope you enjoy the fridge." He patted the top of the refrigerator as if it were a pet, then turned to Dan. "Shall we?"

"Sure," Dan said and took one last look at the roses for good measure.

At the front door, Alan grudgingly shook hands with the deliverymen to send them on their way. He felt relief at having gotten rid of them, but unfortunately his troubles were far from over. He noticed, as the two men exited the house, that both of them dragged their feet across the threshold of the front door as if they had gimp legs. An instant later the delivery truck started up and sped off, and all the while Alan remained in the doorway glowering at the boot prints on the black aluminum threshold and at the scuffed and cracked rubber weather-stripping that previously had been pristine. His eyes moved from the weather-stripping to the damaged doorframe and back again. He was beside himself. In fact, if he had had a weaker constitution, he might have wept—and all because of the carelessness of a couple of workmen, the very thought of whom now made him sick. It seemed like every time such people came to the house, they created more problems than they solved. They were like bulls in a china shop, with no respect for other people's property. Only a few weeks before, a painter painting in Alan's living room had knocked a clock off the wall, shattering it to pieces. The time before that some landscapers had cut the wire connecting the outdoor intercom to his landline. In neither case did he receive an apology, and in both cases, when confronted, the perpetrators denied all wrongdoing, leaving him to foot the bill for the damage. This time, with the refrigerator, the damage was slight in comparison, but again he was left to deal with the aftermath himself. He was particularly irked at the thought of the effort it would take to complete the repairs. In addition to wasting time fixing the doorframe, he would have to waste time replacing parts of the threshold. His list of grievances for the dispatcher, it occurred to him, was growing by the minute.

He doubted the situation could get any worse. But upon entering the kitchen to ensure all was well with the refrigerator, he saw for the first time what he had been too distracted to see before: the imprint of a hand left by John the deliveryman smack-dab in the middle of the refrigerator door. Even more aggravating, the shape of the handprint was mildly obscene, the middle finger jutting nearly an inch above the index and ring fingers. The positioning of the fingers was no more than a freak occurrence, but for some reason Alan took it personally. He was tempted, purely out of spite, to call the dispatcher again and have the refrigerator returned. But he realized that that would involve all the accompanying nonsense of delivering another refrigerator, including potentially a repetition of the two-hour wait, not to mention more workmen wreaking God-knew-what further havoc on the house. He supposed he had no choice but to keep the current refrigerator and to do his best to remove the handprint.

His first thought was to the clean the stainless steel using dish soap and water. He had used such a method before on other appliances, such as to remove grease from the kitchen hood, and it worked just fine. So he saw no reason now—as he lightly dampened a paper towel under the kitchen faucet and added a dollop of liquid soap—not to do the same thing with the refrigerator. All that happened upon applying the soap, however, was to make matters worse. Instead of removing the handprint, the soap simply smeared it, and the subsequent buffing he did using a dry paper towel smeared it even more. The result was a grotesque shape that looked like a strange alien hand with elongated fingers. Alan thought he was imagining things. He took a step back from the refrigerator for a change of perspective, to get a different angle of light. But no, it had not been a trick of light; even there, a few feet away, the handprint was as plain as day, its creepy, claw-like fingers outrageously flipping him the bird.

He was unsure what to do next, although he knew he could not leave the refrigerator as it was. If he were to, he would be certain to lose a night's sleep; it would drive him nuts to have a blemish on the refrigerator before it was even a day old. As he stood there considering his options, he remembered the complementary bottle of stainless-steel cleaner he had received with the kitchen hood a few years back. He had never used any of it before, but he figured now was as good a time as any because his next appointment was not for another hour, after his lunch break was over. He went to the pantry and rummaged through a bin of cleaning supplies. Near the bottom of the bin was a small eight-ounce bottle of stainless-steel cleaner. He took it into the kitchen to get a better look. The marketing on the bottle claimed nothing short of a miracle: its "streak-free formula," it suggested, could clean food residue, fingerprints, and kitchen grease with equal effectiveness. Alan made special note of the part about fingerprints. The fact that the manufacturer had anticipated a problem similar to the one he was now facing boded well. The cleaner, he thought, was sure to do the trick. He followed the product's instructions to the letter, applying the self-proclaimed magical liquid using a soft rag and then buffing it out. The process took nearly five minutes, but by the end of it, there was little to show for his effort, as the definition of the handprint had hardly changed. If anything, the appearance of the refrigerator was worse, the cleaner having left faint horizontal streaks, contrary to the promises on the bottle's labeling.

Alan speculated that perhaps the cleaner had gone bad. He did not know if such a thing could happen, but it did not seem completely out of the realm of possibility. The only way to confirm his theory would be to try other stainless-steel cleaning products on the refrigerator, as well. He would have to go to the hardware store to see what he could find. It would take him more time than he had at the moment, but he simply could not wait until the evening or the weekend. He knew perfectly well that if he *were* to wait, he would spend the rest of the afternoon fretting, which would do a disservice both to himself and his patients, who deserved no less than his full attention during their therapy sessions. Without a second thought, he called his secretary and asked to her cancel the remainder of the day's appointments. An emergency had come up, he told her—which to his mind was no exaggeration. In a twisted sort of logic, he viewed the cancelations as tantamount to treating his customers as sovereign, and it no longer mattered to him that something as mundane as a refrigerator had interfered with the smooth operation of his psychiatry practice. His primary concern now was that he had a mission to accomplish.

Half an hour later he returned from the hardware store with a small arsenal of stainless-steel cleaning products: two in liquid form, a canister of wipes, and an industrial-strength spray. As if preparing for battle, he lined up the products on the kitchen counter in the order in which he intended to use them. He ogled his stash of cleaners as if mentally rubbing his hands together, his eyes intimating that he would return the refrigerator to its original state if it were the last thing he would do. But his confidence was misplaced. One at a time he opened the four cleaning products and tried them out. For the better part of an hour he applied, buffed, re-applied, and buffed again the supposed wonder-working chemicals, all to no avail. He was miffed. In total the cleaners had cost him upwards of $75, but they were not worth the metal and plastic they were contained in. While it was true that after the repeated applications, the handprint was only a shadow of its former self, it and the protruding middle finger were still visible. It also seemed as if the different chemical formulas of the four products had reacted badly to each other, the result of which was a cloudy film on the door of the refrigerator that made it appear ancient. With a look of disgust on his face, Alan spent another fifteen minutes applying soap and water to the refrigerator and buffing it several more times. But it made no difference: the faded handprint and the cloudy film were permanent fixtures.

Now there was no reasonable course of action left to him except to quit. He had come full circle, and, ridiculously, more than once. He was so angry at his stupidity, he could have spit. What galled him more than anything else was how he himself was largely to blame for the current state of the refrigerator. With the threshold and the doorframe, others could be blamed. But with the refrigerator, even if it *had* been John the deliveryman who started it all, the botched attempts at removing the handprint were his fault and his fault alone. It was almost more than he could bear to think that his own actions had led to the marring of an object so prominently on display in his house. Its presence would be a constant reminder of the absurdity of what he had done. He stared with loathing at the refrigerator. *Just look at the damned thing*, he thought. He wondered how a product labeled stainless steel could become so inordinately dirty. The very term was a misnomer. Maybe the surface was impervious to rust, but certainly it was not "stainless" as he understood the word.

Or was it? In his mind was a nagging scintilla of doubt. What if he had somehow misused the various cleaning products, and the refrigerator was as stainless as advertised? He was not yet ready to believe that the mess he had created was irreversible. He went back to the kitchen counter and methodically read the four products' instructions. One of the liquid cleaners indicated that the chemicals should be given ample time to dry on the surface of the appliance before buffing. This could be where he had gone wrong: he may not have given the products enough time to work their magic. He barely had the energy to test the cleaners again, but even the remotest possibility of success would make it worthwhile.

He was on the verge of once more running the gauntlet of cleaners when he checked himself. It suddenly struck him that only a fool would fall into the same trap over and over. The thought reminded him of a saying he once heard. It was on the tip of his tongue. He remembered something about the saying's having been falsely attributed to Albert Einstein or Benjamin Franklin or some other equally famous person. How did it go again? He strained for a while, delving deeply into the recesses of his memory, until finally it came to him. It was a layman's definition of insanity, which went something like this: to repeat the same action over and over again and each time expect a different result. He laughed to himself upon recalling the definition. He knew it was not clinically sound, but he did not care because it amused him. For the moment at least, he failed to fully appreciate the definition's relevance to his own recent behavior. These days he rarely managed to see in himself what he invariably saw in others.

Remembrance

THIS PAST DECEMBER I got it into my head to go solo quail hunting out at the Santa Rita Experimental Range south of Tucson, where I now live. I hadn't gone hunting for nearly a decade, not since before my father died, and I think I had the vague notion that by taking up the sport again, I would be paying tribute to his memory. Growing up in South Dakota, I was never very interested in hunting, even though it was the ideal place for it, Redfield once being the "pheasant capital of the world," and even though my father was an avid outdoorsman. Before I was big enough to wield a gun, I would tag along with him on a hunt every once in a while, but somehow a passion for chasing and killing things failed to take a permanent hold. Back then I was more interested in basketball and in girls. But attitudes and perspectives can change. The older I get, it seems, the more I value what I used to consider the countrified experiences of my past, such as the times I went hunting with my father.

The Range is located off I-19, sandwiched between Sahuarita and Madera Canyon. It is managed by the University of Arizona and is open to the general public for hunting. I had some time off this past December, and so I decided to check out the foothills of the Santa Ritas on the northeastern edge of the Range. The unseasonably warm winter we were having meant that the likelihood I would run into a covey of Gambel's or other quail (they tend to huddle together when the weather turns cold) would be slim, but I figured it would be worth a shot anyway. If nothing else, I would get some exercise and see a bit of scenery.

I was, besides, eager to try my hand at hunting quail, regardless of whether I would successfully bag one. Gambel's quail are a conspicuous feature of the Sonoran-desert landscape. They thrive even in urban areas like Tucson. On walks or bike rides in my neighborhood, I often see entire families of them: a brood of five or six chicks in the wake of their parents, scurrying through the underbrush. Occasionally one of the adult males gets spooked as I go by, and with a flash of black and russet, the comma-shaped plume jutting from its head, it catapults into the air, making a chip-chip sound and moving so fast its wingbeats are audible. Whenever this happens, I get an irresistible itch in my trigger finger, an itch I thought a trip out to the Range might satisfy.

I got an early start, packing up the Subaru with hunting gear, food, and water. It was only seven o'clock by the time I left the house, but already it was relatively warm, at around 50 degrees. It occurred to me that the orange fleece and fingerless wool gloves I was wearing would have to be shed before the day was through.

At the Range just west of the foothills is a side road paralleling a wash that channels rainwater during the monsoon season. This seemed as good a place as any for me to hunt. There wouldn't be any water now, of course, but the quail might congregate nearby simply because the foothills received slightly more rainfall than the surrounding areas. I parked the Subaru along the side road, in what little shade there was under a mesquite tree, and felt a twinge of exhilaration as I did so. I had never been to the Range before, let alone hunted it, yet the motions I was going through seemed to strike a chord, as if I were returning to an old haunt. The high desert of Arizona was a far cry from the plains of South Dakota, but apparently hunting was hunting, irrespective of venue. I got out of the car, harnessed my canteen, and loaded five shells into my Benelli 12-gauge. One shell probably would have been enough, but I couldn't be certain of how well I would shoot.

I had to pass a row of paloverde trees to get to the wash. Once there, the going was tougher than I expected. The wash was dry and sandy, and the ground beneath my feet kept giving way. About thirty yards in, I decided to veer off and cut through some shrubs between the wash and the base of a hill. If I could skirt the hill, I thought, I could walk on firmer ground and maybe also scare up a quail or two. The birds were unlikely to roost out in the open on the wash itself anyway, and I didn't mind trekking through rougher terrain. I kept telling myself that physical hardships were part and parcel of the hunting experience.

I am not sure what triggered the memory, but as I gingerly made my way through a thicket of creosote bushes alongside the hill, my shotgun at port arms, I suddenly thought of the last hunt my father and I went on together. It was about two months before he died, in the middle of February, and he had invited me to go pheasant hunting at a ranch near Belle Fourche for the third time that season. It had been ages since he went hunting so much. But then at the time, he knew he was dying, and not surprisingly he became nostalgic, pining for the things he experienced as a kid. In fact, not long after he learned that the melanoma had worked its way inexorably through his lymph nodes and into his vital organs, he started blowing his savings on Gene Autry paraphernalia and other collectibles associated with his childhood from the Fifties. And he also took up hunting again.

February wasn't the best time of year to go pheasant hunting, but the Belle Fourche ranch stocked pheasants. So it wouldn't be too difficult for my father and me to shoot our limit in short order. Hopeful of our success, we arrived at the ranch at around eight o'clock. It was a cold and blustery day. A three-inch blanket of snow lay on the ground; whorls of powder, twisting and turning, moved across the open fields surrounding the ranch house.

Mr. Atkins, the ranch owner, was waiting for us outside the barn when we pulled up. "Good morning," he called out, giving us an appreciative look as we stepped from my father's Blazer. He turned his rotund body and in a single movement of his head took in the entirety of our surroundings—the azure sky, the blinding white snow, the fields of withered cornstalks in the distance—the meaning of which was perfectly clear: that, despite the wind and chill, it was a good day for a hunt. Then, without further ado, he headed toward the house and gestured for us to follow. Like most South Dakotans, Mr. Atkins was a man of few words.

The three of us stomped the snow from our boots on the entryway rug. A fire was burning in the fireplace of the great room, and my father and I silently stood by it while Mr. Atkins prepared our paperwork and the tags for the six birds we expected to shoot. As we waited, I couldn't help scrutinizing the décor of the room. It was the stereotypical ranch house, with giant rusted-out wagon wheels propped up against wooden pillars. Adorning nearly every square inch of available space on the walls were animal taxidermy and Frederic Remington prints. The word tacky came irrepressibly to mind.

I was about to make a snide remark concerning the contents of the room when Mrs. Atkins emerged from the kitchen and offered us coffee, which we gladly accepted. She came back a minute later with two steaming-hot cups of it. "This will warm you up," she said, smiling. She seemed to want to talk because she lingered after she gave us our coffee. "How long are you back in Rapid City for?" she asked me.

"Only for the weekend," I said, my lips hovering above the rim of my cup. I was still living in Los Angeles at the time, working as an economist in a high-stress environment, and so it was hard to get away.

"You must love your dad a lot," she said and looked at my father knowingly. Even she knew he was dying of cancer.

I didn't know what to say, so I just nodded and smiled. I *did* love my dad, but I couldn't tell her the truth, which was that I had come to see him for the third time in as many months mainly out of a sense of filial duty. Ever since my parents' divorce, twelve years earlier, my relationship with my father had been strained. And even when I was a kid, he and I were never very close—not that he was fully to blame, though, with a wife and five children vying for his attention.

There was an awkward silence as Mrs. Atkins waited for a response from me that would never come.

Thankfully my father intervened. "It's amazing he's come to see me at all," he said, gesturing in my direction, "given his busy schedule. And his wife is Asian, so he has to split his vacation time between me in Rapid, his mom in Tucson, and his in-laws overseas. Every summer they travel for a month to visit his wife's family. He hardly has time for anything else, but he still manages to see me." As my father said all this, he had a gleam in his eyes. For some reason it always made him proud to discuss with friends and acquaintances what he viewed as my exotic experiences, as if they were a positive reflection on him personally.

I never liked it when he spoke this way. The comments themselves were harmless; it was the tone in which he said them that irritated me. We had been estranged for too long for him to pretend we were closer than we actually were. His claim on experiences that were mine made me feel resentful and gave me the urge to insult his intelligence. To Mrs. Atkins I said, "When he says my wife is Asian, he really means she's Sri Lankan. Most Sri Lankans don't like being associated with neighboring India, let alone lumped together with the fifty-odd other Asian countries." It wasn't much of an insult, but it was enough.

"Yes … Sri Lankan," my father faltered, his face turning red.

Mrs. Atkins gave me a dirty look as if to say, "Cut your dad some slack."

Almost ten years have passed since that conversation with Mrs. Atkins, and still it remains for me a defining moment in my relationship with my father. I sometimes find myself replaying in my mind the details of the exchange, internalizing the pang he must have felt on being insulted. Obviously I can't change the past, but in retrospect, I wish I *had* cut him some slack. I am ashamed of how petty my concerns were at the time. My father was dying and all I could do in response was to criticize him for a loose ethnic reference. Plus, I never did apologize; I was too self-centered, too caught up in the moment. I suspect it was regret about this, and regret in general, that later made me receptive to commemorating my father's death anniversary, which I have done now every April 16th for going on nine years. I originally adopted the custom because of my wife Rajivi, who is an orthodox Buddhist. Normally each summer, after the onset of the Yala monsoon, she and I take a trip to her ancestral home in Sri Lanka. But the year after my father died, a confluence of events caused us to travel during

April instead. While we were there, Rajivi suggested we arrange a *dānē*, or almsgiving, to be administered by local priests at her parents' place. I was still grieving then, even a year on, and so I readily agreed to it.

A *dānē* is an elaborate affair. I won't soon forget the one at my in-laws'. It all comes back to me now with such clarity: the rich saffron of the monks' robes; the lit candles; the frangipani flowers afloat in water-filled stone vases; the wisps of smoke rising from joss sticks and the attendant smell of sandalwood; the soothing hum of the monks' chanting voices. Typically the proceedings last for over an hour. After a small group of novices and young bhikkhus seat themselves on floor pillows—frozen in the lotus position like an art-gallery exhibition of Buddha statues—the ceremony begins. The head priest recites a series of arcane Pali verses to confer merit on the deceased. When the chanting ends, food is served to the priests. This is followed by other rituals, including a *pirit* ceremony in which *pirit* thread (white string that bestows a blessing on its wearer) is tied to the wrist of each layperson in attendance. Only then do the priests depart.

That morning at my in-laws', I remember feeling relieved at the ceremony's end, not because it was over but because it gave me a sense of closure on my father's death. It may have had something to do with the elegance of the *dānē* ceremony itself, which is meant to bring good karma to someone reborn in their next life. Whether I believed in rebirth or not, I could be happy in the knowledge that thoughts and prayers had gone out to my father wherever his "soul" then resided. To me it was the act of remembrance that mattered, not the metaphysics of the afterlife.

The first few years after that initial *dānē*, I religiously kept up, in my own way, the tradition of honoring my father's death anniversary, like clockwork each spring sending a donation to the hospice in South Dakota that cared for him so graciously during his final days. But I have to admit I have grown lax of late in my observation of the occasion. I have long since stopped donating to the hospice, and more recently my remembrance of my father on April 16th has been limited to a brief moment of silence on my way to work. I don't know why—it is only natural, after all, to move on with one's life after losing someone—but I have started feeling guilty about my apparent lapses. Perhaps it is because the ten-year anniversary of his death is just around the corner. Or maybe it is because I am becoming increasingly aware of my own mortality. My father died young, at the age of fifty-seven, as did his mother before him, and so if I follow in their footsteps, my own time isn't too far off, less than a decade and a half away, in fact. It pains me to think that my own son might one day forget me like I seem to be forgetting *my* father.

Mrs. Atkins was still glaring at me moments later when her husband joined us by the fire. He must not have overheard any of our earlier conversation because he acted as if nothing were amiss. "If you're ready," he said pleasantly, "we can head out."

My father and I handed our half-drunk coffee to Mrs. Atkins and thanked her, then followed Mr. Atkins to the door. Neither of us said a word or so much as looked at each other as we did so.

Outside, the weather had taken a turn for the worse. The wind was blowing more intensely, and although the sky overhead was clear, in the distance a thick layer of dark clouds threatened snow. I remarked on this to Mr. Atkins. He wasn't too perturbed by the prospect of a storm, however. In fact, he said it augured well for our hunt. Colder air and fresh snow would make it easier for his dog Sheila to track birds. Not that she needed any help, he pointed out. He often joked, as now, that she was so good at what she did she could track a white cat in a blizzard, or something to that effect. I didn't doubt it. He had good reason to be confident in her abilities. Besides being incredibly fit—one of those field-bred black Labs with the powerful physique of a Thoroughbred horse—she was the best gundog I had ever seen. Watching her in action was enough to take your breath away. The last time my father and I went hunting on the Atkins ranch, she did this curling maneuver in a cornfield that sent three roosters bursting from the cut stalks not twenty feet from our faces. We were so startled at the time that neither of us got a shot off. Later, when we asked Mr. Atkins about it, he told us that Sheila developed the strategy entirely on her own. "She's a natural-born hunter," he said with a grin.

As we approached the barn now to retrieve Sheila for the hunt, we could hear her whining and pawing at the door. She was always like that: more keen to get started than we were, her body thrumming with tension in anticipation of the chase. The instant Mr. Atkins opened the barn door, she came bounding out, using every ounce of discipline in her body to keep from jumping onto us.

"Hello, girl," I said, kneeling down and petting her. I didn't much care for dogs but gladly made an exception for Sheila. To my mind she was a breed apart.

I could tell from her hurried movements where her priorities lay. Hardly had she licked my hand in a mutual show of affection than she was off, leading Mr. Atkins and my father and me toward the nearest cornfield, her enthusiasm in no way blunted by the wind and cold.

We hadn't yet reached our destination before she became birdy. Her otter tail began to wag spasmodically, and then, in a complete u-turn, she became placid, her pace slowing to a measured crawl like a big cat stalking prey. She did something similar on our last hunt; according to Mr. Atkins, it suggested that whatever she was on to was unlikely to run. She must have been only a few yards away from her quarry now because her body suddenly went rigid.

All that was left for us to do was to decide who would take the shot. I could fairly guess who it would be. When it came to hunting, my father was never selfish. He got a kind of vicarious joy out of watching others shoot. It also apparently engendered in him a camaraderie that melted away any grudges he might have held. I could see something of the sort written on his features now as he looked at me to indicate that the bird Sheila tracked down was mine for the taking if I wanted it. I did. I thumbed the safety on my 12-guage and as quietly as I could sneaked up behind Sheila. I was just parallel with her when I saw the bird hunkered down in a patch of snow-matted needlegrass. It was a juvenile rooster, and it had its back to us; the motley colors of its head and neck iridesced in the sunlight. At first I thought it was dead because it didn't budge, even though Sheila and I were practically standing on top of it. But then I saw it move, its head turning almost imperceptibly to take me in askance with a single eye. It blinked several times but held tight. I was dumbfounded. I could think of only two explanations: either it thought it wouldn't be seen if it stayed motionless, or else it was in a state of tonic immobility, like a rabbit when it feels threatened by a predator.

Whatever the case may have been, Sheila was getting impatient. She looked up at me pleadingly, then back to the bird, emitting from deep within her throat an odd gurgling noise, a cross between a growl and a whine. I didn't know how else to scare up the bird, so I simply stomped my foot on the ground. Instantly, with a loud raspy cackle, it took to the air, its wings grotesquely distorted by the violence of its effort. At about eight feet up, it stopped its upward trajectory, released some whitewash in its wake, and began to glide. I was presented with an easy straightaway shot. In a single motion I shouldered my gun and pulled the trigger. There was a sudden explosion of tail feathers, followed by an aerial summersault or two. Before I could mark where the bird went down, Sheila dashed to retrieve it. Presently she brought it back to hand. I removed a glove and held the bird for a moment, feeling its dead weight and its warm and velvety feathers. Then with a flourish I stowed it in my game bag.

"Good shot," my father said. He came over and patted me on the back. "You get better every time we come out."

Mr. Atkins nodded in agreement.

I didn't contradict them, even though it really was an easy shot; I would take what compliments I could get.

A few minutes later we were in a line formation—my father on the right, Mr. Atkins in the middle, and me on the left—chest deep in desiccated, snow-covered cornstalks, which were so stiff and brittle to the touch, they rattled every time we brushed up against them. Sheila was already ten yards ahead of us, making her way from row to row to get the birds to flush. But they were having none of it and instead were running. Every now and then we would see a rooster scurrying up one of the rows of cornstalks to keep its distance from Sheila. Finally Mr. Atkins sent her to the other end of the field to act as a blocker. He put a thumb and middle finger in his mouth and whistled, and immediately she moved laterally out of the cornstalks, then sprinted the length of the field. Within seconds she was obediently waiting for us to drive the birds to *her* instead of the other way around.

What happened next was a blur. We couldn't have been more than a dozen paces from Sheila's end of the field, ready to give up on what seemed like an ill-fated pheasant drive, when suddenly she let out a single, portentous yelp, and just like that, with minimal cover in which to hide, a couple of hens and four or five roosters surged from the cornstalks between us and Sheila. Bedlam ensued as bird after bird towered up— some flying this way, some that. The rooster nearest me flushed so close I could feel its wing-wind on my face. It ascended maniacally, its tail feathers whipping and billowing. I nearly fell over trying to mount my gun. By the time I steadied myself and pointed the barrel straight up into the air, the bird was already leveling out its flight. I fired, hitting nothing but air. I completely lost my composure after that. The next thing I knew I was letting fly three Hail-Mary shots in quick succession, the shells going off like machinegun fire. The bird went unscathed. I watched helplessly as it flew out of gun range, my Benelli dangling at my side in a limp, three-fingered trail carry. Standing there in a daze, I heard a crack from my father's 20-gauge and peripherally saw a rooster fall from the sky about twenty yards to my right. I turned to take stock of what just happened, and there my father was, poised like a professional skeet shooter, drawing a bead on a second rooster that was even farther afield than the last one. I heard another crack from his 20-gauge and saw another bird fall from the sky. Two shots, two kills. It was incredible. Even with terminal cancer, he hadn't lost his touch.

I would have congratulated him, but I was still rankling from my piss-poor shooting. I tramped over to his side of the field, my head held down in shame. "I don't know what happened," I said, continuing to brood. I was pathetically amateurish compared to him, and I knew it now more than ever.

He knew it too, but he encouraged me all the same. "The day's still young," he said. "A few more shots and you'll work out the kinks."

I wasn't so sure. Besides, the amount of time left in the day was the least of our concerns. "We'll need luck of *another* kind," I said, glancing doubtfully at the looming clouds. I wanted nothing more than to redeem my earlier shooting, but at the same time I didn't want my father to overexert himself. In the end I put the onus on him. "Do you think you'll be up to braving the weather," I asked, "if it turns foul?"

The look in his eyes suggested he had only just gotten started. "I'm game if you are," he said like a venturesome teenager.

I probably should have made an executive decision at that point to call it a day, but my father's enthusiasm was infectious. I said excitedly, "I didn't come all the way from LA to be deterred by a little snow." Then I turned to Mr. Atkins to get his take on the matter. "Any objections to our continuing?"

He shrugged. "It's your call."

Thinking out loud, I said, "We *are* still three birds shy of our limit."

"That settles it, then," my father said. "We soldier on."

As it happened, the next cornfield on our itinerary was oddly L-shaped so that an organized pheasant drive would be difficult. We decided to traverse it separately, similar to the last two occasions my father and I were here. My father and Sheila went one way, and I and Mr. Atkins went another. Barely a minute after we did so, Mr. Atkins and I kicked up a single rooster. It came rocketing by, just above the cornstalks, moving from right to left. In a flash I snapped my gun to the ready position and fired. The bird didn't miss a wingbeat. I cursed under my breath. I was tempted to give up then and there, but just as I was about to, I had an epiphany. I lowered my gun and raised my head, re-establishing visual contact with the target, which was now about fifteen yards out. Slowly I rotated my body and at the same time shouldered my gun and pointed the muzzle several inches in front of the conspicuous white neck ring. I pulled the trigger and immediately the bird buckled and dropped.

"Nice recovery!" Mr. Atkins hollered from behind me.

"I was smart enough to lead it the second time," I responded, not realizing the import of my words until afterward. Somehow intuitively I figured out what the problem was with my shooting: I had been aiming directly at the target, regardless of its position, and so whenever a passing shot presented itself, I would consistently miss behind it. I suspected my father had something to do with this discovery. Just seeing him in action likely rubbed off on me. My only regret was that he wasn't around to witness the result. I said, "It's too bad Dad wasn't here."

"Maybe next time," Mr. Atkins said vaguely and left it at that.

But there never was a next time, with my father present or otherwise. Mr. Atkins and I combed the remainder of our section of the cornfield without flushing another bird. Disappointed, we headed for the rendezvous point, where the L-shaped cornfield abutted the creek that ran through Mr. Atkins' property. We expected my father and Sheila to already be there, as they clearly hadn't fared any better than we had; not a single shot had been heard from their direction of the field. Upon our arrival, however, they were nowhere to be seen. For several minutes we stood around waiting, doing our best to stay warm in the worsening weather. As the sun disappeared behind a cloud, the temperature seemed to drop ten degrees, although our inactivity no doubt contributed to this impression. Alternately we blew into our hands and shifted our weight from leg to leg to increase our blood flow.

I thought nothing of my father's and Sheila's absence until ten minutes elapsed and still they hadn't arrived. Then suddenly I became worried. "What's taking them so long?" I asked impatiently, trying to disguise my concern.

Mr. Atkins was less subtle; he did nothing to hide the look of dread on his face. "I don't want to alarm you," he said, "but maybe we should go search for them. I mean, in your father's condition ..." He didn't complete his thought. I expected him to follow this up with some reassuring words, but instead he proceeded to narrate a story about a widower uncle of his, whom he referred to as the "old man." "My wife and I had invited the old man over for Sunday dinner. We were expecting him by five, but he didn't show. At first we weren't too concerned because he wasn't known for his punctuality. So we waited half an hour before phoning his house. But when we did, there was no answer. We assumed he must still be on his way (the old man hated technology and so didn't have a cell phone), so we waited another half-hour. Still nothing. It was out of character, even for the old man, to be *this* late. Finally I took it upon myself to drive out to his house." At the word "house" Mr. Atkins' voice cracked. He paused for a moment, and in the gathering darkness I saw that his eyes were glistening. "None of the lights were on when I got there. I had this foreboding, an unaccountable ache deep in the pit of my stomach. I considered knocking on the front door but thought better of it. What was the point? With the spare key from under the mat, I opened the door and switched on a light. I didn't have to look any further. On the other side of the living room was the old man, sitting in his La-Z-Boy, eyes wide open and mouth agape, stiff with rigor mortis, pages of the *Rapid City Journal* clutched in one hand."

My heart was in my throat as Mr. Atkins concluded his story. Of all the times for the man to become garrulous. He hadn't strung more than four or five consecutive sentences together all day long—and then this. I supposed he meant well, but all he succeeded in doing was to stir up my imagination. Before I could suppress it, I had a vision of my father lying face down in the snow, his arms and legs spread out like an angel's. That was sufficient for me not to dignify Mr. Atkins' comments about his uncle with a response, as it might elicit more of the same. And what he said already was enough. Prior to hearing his story, the thought of my father's death was an abstraction, something indefinite that would happen in the future. But now not only was it real, it was a certainty—if not today, then sometime soon. And I didn't want him to die. "You're right," I said to Mr. Atkins, bringing the conversation back to where it started and ignoring all the intervening verbiage. "We *should* go search for them."

We set out just as it started to snow. Great big flakes of it dropped from the sky one at a time, seemingly in slow motion, whirling earthwards like the boomerang-shaped samaras of a boxelder tree. With the snowfall came a sense of urgency to find my father. Mr. Atkins and I seemed to be in tacit agreement on this; without speaking we hurried toward the fence that bordered the other side of the cornfield. All the while I kept thinking: If my father *did* fall and hurt himself—and is now lying out there somewhere, cold and helpless—how long could he conceivably last?

We weren't five minutes into our search when Mr. Atkins yelled, "There!" I turned my head to see him pointing at the silhouettes of a man and a dog a quarter-mile distant. Through the fluttering snow, I could just make out my father sitting on the ground, his back propped up against a fencepost, and Sheila next to him, licking his face. Soon we were within earshot, and I heard my father say, "No," and saw him playfully push Sheila away. Mr. Atkins and I looked at each other and breathed a collective sigh of relief.

"You had us worried," I said as we came up to them.

My father apologized. "We were tracking a rooster that jumped the fence, and when I tried to scale it myself, I felt lightheaded. I thought I should take a break to be on the safe side." Sitting there on the ground, a dusting of snow on his clothes, he looked cold and exhausted and vulnerable. I suspected he was also in a great deal of pain; more than once he pressed a hand to his abdomen and winced. "I'd rather not quit …" he said and trailed off. He brushed the snow from his beanie and from the shoulders of his coat, then grabbed onto the fencepost and started to hoist himself up. His breathing, I noticed, was labored. I reached out to give him a hand, to help him in the least way I could, but he shooed me away. "I'm not *that* decrepit," he said.

I backed away, keeping silent. I knew not to take his brusqueness personally; he was reacting to the cancer, not to me. I cradled my gun in the crook of my elbow and watched him struggle to his feet. He seemed determined to be defiant to the last. I wondered whether I would have the same fortitude when faced with my own death. I very much doubted it. My father was made of sterner stuff. The fact that he went hunting at all, instead of convalescing, was testimony to that.

I won't pretend the entire sequence of events of my last hunt with my father came back to me successively out at the Range that day this past December. It was more like the fastforwarding of a film, snippets here and there flashing through my mind, some of the images just below the threshold of my awareness. I was thinking of that last image in particular—of my father propped up on the fencepost in the falling snow, refusing to let his illness get the better of him— as I emerged from the thicket of creosote bushes, the Arizona sun bearing down on me. I unzipped my fleece and squinted into the sun and felt strangely contented. For the first time I had an inkling of what it was for my father that gave bird hunting such a special allure. It wasn't just the excitement of the chase and the demonstration of skill in wingshooting. It had as much, if not more, to do with communing with nature and the making of memories—or the reliving of memories, as the case was now. For another hour or so I trekked through the foothills of the Santa Ritas, navigating rugged draws and avoiding cacti and thorny succulents at every third step. Midway through the hunt, right before I turned back to the Subaru, I reached the top of a hill and was descending into a small ravine when I stumbled onto a white-tailed deer browsing in the shade of an acacia tree. It was a juvenile buck, so close I could see its antler pedicles. We both froze, staring bewilderingly at each other. I might have stood there gazing at the deer indefinitely if it hadn't been so skittish. With a sudden flag of its tail, exposing the white underside, it pranced up the bank of the ravine opposite me, stopped for a moment to look back, then disappeared over a ridge. That was as close as I got to a game animal that day; the quail were conspicuously absent. I probably should have been disappointed by this, but I wasn't. I came away feeling the day had been well spent, even without food for my table or a notch in my belt.

Inglorious Carnage

NO ONE WAS MORE VOCAL than Mrs. Parks about the recent explosion of ground squirrels in the neighborhood. She was the president of the homeowners' association and for weeks had been hounding people to address the problem, which she insisted was due to the previous year's unseasonably warm winter. She never failed to complain whenever she had a chance. Today, on the street outside her house, she happened to bump into two of her neighbors, Mr. Douglas and Mr. Krieg, while retrieving the mail. The first words out of her mouth were a sardonic remark about the weather. She admitted that last winter Tucson had been a paradise on earth, but she sounded more irritated than pleased by this. In her characteristic cynicism, she said nothing good comes without a cost, at the very mention of which her voice became grave, as if she were referring to the effects of an Ebola outbreak. She stopped for a moment to gauge the neighbors' reactions. They met her gaze with faces of stone, but she was undeterred. Shading her eyes with a hand, she peered up into the blistering June sun, then turned back to the two men with a look of utter disgust on her face. "Now we're paying the price," she said vaguely and stood there staring with unease at the myriad holes and mounds dotting the common areas along the street.

Mr. Douglas needed no prompting from Mrs. Parks. He was livid about the "little bastards," as he so peevishly referred to the ground squirrels. He called for immediate action. "Something's got to be done. At first I thought they were cute, but that was before they started destroying my driveway." His voice wavered. Then he said, "See what I mean?" as he pointed with a trembling hand toward his house. Near the garage, where the squirrels had excavated a network of tunnels, several sections of paving stones were completely caved in, appearing to the untrained eye as if they had been hit by an earthquake.

Upon seeing the damage, Mr. Krieg guffawed, his dark sense of humor getting the better of him. "Good Lord," he said, slapping Mr. Douglas on the back. "I had no idea it was as bad as *that*." He was not exaggerating his ignorance. He could be oblivious in matters in which he was not directly concerned, a fault his wife Eileen was constantly berating him for. Now, as if seeing things for the first time, he took in the dire state of his neighbors' yards. Entrance after entrance to the squirrels' burrows lined the gravel paths skirting the street. He was reminded of the prairie-dog colony he had seen on a recent trip to the Desert Museum. He wondered how the squirrels had done it all so quickly. It seemed to him that they had tunneled their way through the neighborhood practically overnight.

"So what do you propose we do about it?" asked Mrs. Parks, frowning at Mr. Krieg as if *he* were somehow to blame.

But he did not respond. He continued to look in disbelief at the squirrel mounds, even as Mrs. Parks' question hung on the air like an accusation.

In the coming days, Maximus Krieg, as the secretary and lowest-ranking officer of the HOA, was tasked with finding a solution to the rodent problem. He was the logical person for the job: he was a school teacher; it was summer break; and he had an abundance of time on his hands. Or so the thinking went. All the HOA members agreed that the first priority was to "deal with" the ground squirrels. Nobody had any illusions about what that meant, as capturing the squirrels live was out of the question because of the expense. Only one pest-control company in town had a license for squirrels, and that was restricted to live-trapping and relocating them, at $100 an hour. Mr. Douglas said he did not care about the money, but the other HOA members, including Max, balked. The bills would rack up fast, and what if after several hundred dollars in payments, there was only a negligible reduction in the numner of squirrels? Someone suggested poisoning them as a cheap alternative, but Eileen and others were concerned about the effect the poison might have on animals up the food chain. Among other things, the neighborhood had a resident family of Harris' hawks, and if even one of them were inadvertently killed, no one, least of all Eileen, would be able to forgive themselves.

As so often happens in deliberations by committee, the HOA's discussions ended in indecision. Max was left simply to "explore other options" and to report back at the next official HOA meeting in two months' time. But he had no intention of standing idly by while the squirrels wreaked havoc. The state of Mr. Douglas' driveway, as funny as it was, seemed to foreshadow things to come. It was one thing, Max thought, for someone else's property to be destroyed; it was quite another for it to happen to his. For days, after seeing the damage inflicted by the squirrels, apocalyptic visions rose up in his mind: his yard becoming a veritable Gaza Strip of tunnels, his own driveway collapsing. He had even heard—from where, he could not remember—of ground squirrels tunneling under garages and ruining foundations (it was not so farfetched; he had heard of crazier things happening). That was all he needed. It would mean thousands of dollars in repairs. To avoid this, he started patrolling his yard every morning for signs of squirrels. All he ever found were what appeared to be rat holes, but he took no chances. With a shovel he cleared away the gravel and dug up and buried the runways and underground trenches for as far as he could unearth them. After a week of frenzied digging, his yard looked like it had been worked over haphazardly by a plow. There had to be a better way.

Then an idea came to him. It was so simple it was ingenious: he would buy one of those scoped air rifles and hunt the squirrels down. He called Arizona Game and Fish to find out whether it was legal to fire a pellet gun within the city limits. The only restriction was that air rifles could not exceed 0.30 caliber, which made the issue moot because most were barely half that size. He saw this as a green light to proceed. That very afternoon he went online and bought a Crosman TR77, a 250-count container of "Destroyer" pellets, and a gun case. During and after the purchase, he could hardly contain his excitement. He felt like a child awaiting the arrival of a new toy.

Coincidentally, Mr. Douglas had the same thought about shooting the squirrels. The day after the Crosman had been ordered, he sent an e-mail to Eileen (she was co-president of the HOA along with Mrs. Parks) suggesting half-seriously, half-facetiously that he and Max buy scoped air rifles and start sniping the squirrels. Eileen showed Max the e-mail, unaware a rifle was already on its way. "What do you think?" she asked dubiously. The thought of Mr. Douglas and her husband toting rifles around the neighborhood made her mildly squeamish. "Shall we at least consider it? We seem to be running out of options."

Max pretended it was the first he had considered such a thing. In the clear light of day, now that the novelty of buying the gun had worn off, he was embarrassed at having come up with the idea himself. How exactly he had intended to explain the postal delivery of a Crosman was unclear, but the fortuitous e-mail from Mr. Douglas gave him a way out. "I don't know," Max said in response to Eileen's question, feigning misgiving about the use of a gun. "Although ..." He was silent for a moment, as if deep in thought. "... maybe it *isn't* such a bad idea."

The package with the Crosman arrived a few days later. Max carried it into the living room and removed the packaging. He found the gun surprisingly heavy, weighing as it did more than six pounds, but its sophistication compensated for its weight. He held it up to the light: black from stock to muzzle, it was so menacing-looking it could have passed as a police tactical rifle. He felt a tingling sensation in his spine as he mounted the scope and lined up the crosshairs on nothing in particular out a window. It would do nicely, he thought. In fact, it was all but a certainty now, with a rifle in hand, that the squirrels were doomed. He never did anything in half measures. If it was war the squirrels wanted, it was war they were going to get.

Outside, not five minutes later, Max spotted a squirrel munching a mesquite pod with impunity in front of the Sandbergs' house, catty-corner from his own. He cocked the rifle's break barrel against his thigh, inserted a pellet into the breech, and, like an actor in a western, swung the barrel back into place. The scope had yet to be sighted in, but there was no time for such niceties. He crossed the street and sat down on the curb near Mr. Douglas' driveway, within twenty yards of the offending squirrel. Before lining up the crosshairs, he scanned the street for any sign of the neighbors. It was a weekday, thankfully, at a time when the neighbors were at work, and so no one was about. He breathed a sigh of relief, as he had no desire to explain what he was doing with a rifle. Meanwhile the squirrel had not budged; it went on eating the mesquite pod, completely indifferent to Max's presence. He put the crosshairs on the animal's head, released the safety, took a deep breath, and fired. A puff of dust rose up from the ground six feet in front of the squirrel, followed by a loud thwack against the metal door of the Sandbergs' garage. The squirrel, unscathed, looked around in bewilderment for a second before darting into its burrow.

"Damn it," Max muttered and drew back the safety. Shaking his head, he propped the barrel of the gun onto his shoulder. The only consolation, he thought, was that no one from the neighborhood had heard the ricocheting pellet. Shamefacedly he stood up from the curb. Then he, too, scurried into his house to hide.

He was sure something had been wrong with the rifle's scope; he had never shot so poorly before. True, every gun had a break-in period, but falling six feet short of the target was ridiculous by any measure. So the next day, he set about zeroing the scope. After drawing a makeshift target on a piece of printer paper, he stapled it to a wooden stake, which he drove into the ground in the wash near his house. It was midday and suffocatingly hot. Other than the traffic on Fort Lowell Road and the occasional squeaky trill of a Gila woodpecker, the only sound was that of the cicadas, their songs a distinctively metallic drone in the dry desert heat. He squatted down a few yards from the target in the shade of a mesquite tree. He had a look of deadly earnest on his face. Tilting his bush hat farther back on his head, he drew up the rifle, centered the scope on the bull's eye, and fired. From where he was kneeling, he could see that the pellet had just clipped the outer ring on the bottom-right corner of the target. He had been correct that the scope was off. No wonder he missed the squirrel so miserably the day before. There was no time to waste in fixing the problem. He removed the caps from the elevation and windage dials and, with a flat-edge screwdriver, turned each wheel two clicks up and to the left, respectively. He test fired again, and still the pellet struck more than three inches below and to the right of the center of the target. Several more times he adjusted the wheels until finally the scope was zeroed.

The moment he emerged from the wash he saw two ground squirrels in Mr. Douglas' driveway: one near the curb, the other near the garage. Like the squirrel the day before, these two were indifferent to Max's presence, continuing to forage for mesquite pods even as he sat on the curb, yards from Mr. Douglas' driveway. The squirrels became wary of him only after he had shouldered his rifle. Suddenly the one near the curb scampered to the safety of its burrow but just as quickly returned to the surface, its head sticking up slightly above the dirt mound, as cautiously alert as a sentry. Max seized the opportunity: he centered the crosshairs on the squirrel's head and pulled the trigger. Instantly the squirrel fell to the ground, flopping spasmodically, like a convulsive break dancer. The death throes lasted another minute, and all the while Max kept thinking, *Why won't the thing just die and be done with it?* It all seemed so over the top. When at last there was no longer any movement near the burrow, he went to check on the kill. The mound was spattered with blood, but the squirrel itself was nowhere to be seen. It could not possibly have survived a close-range shot to the head, so where was it? Dead in its burrow? That had to be the case. He would have noticed if it had run off.

As Max ruminated, the other squirrel watched him with an apparent mixture of curiosity and fear. Its head and eyes were just visible from a hole beneath one of the paving stones in Mr. Douglas' driveway. Remaining standing, Max reloaded his gun and took a few measured steps to his right to get a better vantage point. The squirrel did not move, its eyes trained on him suspiciously. He was presented with a perfect, straight-on shot. Without hesitating, he aimed the rifle and fired. The squirrel drew back an inch, convulsed a second, then collapsed under its own weight. *Thank God*, Max thought. *A clean shot.* The image of the last squirrel, its body flailing about, still lingered uncomfortably in his mind, and he was feeling a prick of conscience about it. No animal, not even a pest, deserved unnecessary pain. He wanted the squirrels removed from the neighborhood, but not if it meant torturing them. He was almost ready to throw in the towel when it occurred to him that he had no choice in the matter. He had a job to do. He and the other HOA members had already considered the alternatives, which were too expensive or equally grim. And doing nothing was not an option, either. If he were to leave the squirrels to their own devices, they would destroy *his* driveway next, and *that* he could not allow.

Which of course would mean more killing. Something he was loath to do. But again, what choice did he have? He leaned forward and, like a soldier planting a flag, drove the butt of his rifle into the ground. His situation was untenable. He was damned if he did and damned if he did not. It was fortunate that he had a gun in his hands. He could take out his anger on some unsuspecting rodent, like the squirrel that happened to be relaxing under a fairy duster at the corner of the Dodds' garage, across the street and a good twenty yards from where he now stood. It was a tough shot, with foliage obstructing his view, but he was feeling infallible. He loaded his rifle and fired before he knew what he was doing. There was the sound of breaking branches and metal on rock, after which the squirrel stutter-stepped out from under the shrub, coweringly inched its way to an escape hole, and disappeared. Max went to the hole. On its outer edge was a single spot of blood, no bigger than a pinkie nail. The squirrel had only been nicked. Somehow this made Max's ire dissipate—firing the rifle without killing anything apparently acting as a release—and as a result he was ready to call it quits. He had had enough carnage for one day.

Late the following morning he was getting into his car to drive to the grocery store when he noticed two more ground squirrels. One of them was resting on its haunches in the middle of the Sandbergs' driveway, nonchalantly sunning itself and surveying its surroundings. The other one was foraging closer to the house. "The little bastards," Max said aloud, echoing Mr. Douglas' moniker. He slammed shut his car door and stood staring at the devious rodents with hatred in his eyes. How could there possibly be so many of them? They were everywhere. The shopping, he supposed, would have to wait. He had not intended to hunt today, but clearly he had not realized the direness of the situation. There had to be a whole colony of squirrels in the neighborhood, and the thought of even one of them tunneling under his driveway made him shudder. He would have to act swiftly, and with shock and awe, or he might never be able to keep the animals in check.

Two minutes later he found himself sitting on the curb across the street from the Sandbergs', his rifle pointing at the squirrel in the driveway. Despite his recent shooting, neither of the squirrels had become gunwise; they went about their business as if nothing were awry. He fired. At first the squirrel stood stock-still, but then slowly, its feet remaining firmly planted on the ground, it tilted forward, like a tree being felled. It hit the pavers with its body spread full length. Max assumed it was dead on impact, but shortly afterward it stirred to life. (By this point the other squirrel had vanished.) Zombie-like, it slowly and shakily lifted its upper torso and dragged itself toward a cordia shrub at the edge of the driveway. Centimeter by centimeter it struggled, a faint streak of blood in its wake. On reaching the shrub, it heaved itself onto a lower branch, hung there precariously for an instant, and then flopped down to the ground. Freakishly it clung to life. Max looked on in horror as it did a one-eighty and headed back up the driveway. He would have shot it a second time to put it out of its misery, but he was seized by a sudden paralysis of will. For an uncomfortably long time, the squirrel crawled with what little strength it had left to the Sandbergs' backyard, where, Max was certain, a slow and agonizing death awaited it.

Only after reading *National Geographic* a week later did he have the courage to hunt again. There was an article about elephants encroaching on African villages that were being culled to reduce conflict with humans. Apparently for the culling to be effective in a given locale, the kill rate had to be at least 70 percent; otherwise the animals would come back with a vengeance because of the increased availability of food. It occurred to Max, as he read the article, that the same might be true of the ground squirrels in his neighborhood. To date, he was lucky if he had killed 20 percent of them, and if he did nothing further, in a couple of months, there might be more than when he started. It was a disturbing thought, and one he could not abide.

He resolved to reach the 70-percent cull target and at the

same time avoid a repeat of his last outing. He spent the better part of a Friday afternoon re-sighting the scope of his rifle. A sheet of pellet-riddled printer paper later, he set out to hunt.

The reception he got was unexpected. From his front stoop he heard a high-pitched whistle, and in a flash the handful of squirrels above ground scattered to their respective holes. Somehow during the last week they had become skittish. He would have to up his game if he was going to shoot them now. For a start, he would have to be more patient. He knew that that was something *he* could afford but the squirrels could not; sooner or later they would have to come out of their holes for food. And anyway, it never paid to hurry your shot: either you missed your quarry entirely, or worse, you … But before he could finish his thought, the image of the squirrel with the broken spine crept like a wounded animal into his mind. *Oh God.* If patience was what he needed to avoid *that*, then so be it. Mustering what patience he could, he sat down on the curb in the shade of a mesquite tree and waited. He did not have to wait long. The squirrels' heads began to pop up from their holes one by one, like in a carnival shooter game, until several pairs of tiny eyes were warily fixed on him.

It was then the real carnage began. He started with the squirrel directly across the street. Through the scope of his rifle, he could see the top of its head poking out from a hole beneath one of the Dodds' birds of paradise. His heart pounded as he flipped the safety. He took a deep breath, slowly exhaled. The pellet hit the squirrel right between the eyes. It twitched momentarily at the mouth of the hole before expiring. Scarcely had it done so than Max saw another squirrel rise up from a hole by a saguaro off the Wrights' garage. It stood fully upright, looking at him as if it were curious to know what just happened. This time the force of the pellet was so great it went clean through the squirrel's skull, smacking the saguaro behind it. As its body flung backward and jammed, head first, into an adjacent hole, Max's rifle moved of its own accord and sighted in a third squirrel. Soon it, too, was dead. It lay near the Sandbergs' driveway, its back wedged between two water-meter plates, all four paws absurdly pointing up toward the sky.

So much for patience. There was no stopping Max now. He felt a rush of adrenaline as he glimpsed a fourth squirrel skulking between the Dodds' and the Wrights' garages. He drew a bead on it, but before he could fire, it disappeared into a fifteen-foot length of plastic tubing that had been left out for bulk-garbage pickup. He set down his gun and hurried to the tube. He had to prevent the squirrel from escaping out the other end. He made quick work of lifting the tube and forming it into a ring. The squirrel's claws scraped along the plastic as it slid to the ring's center. Still holding the tubing, Max went to the Dodds' garbage bin and with an index finger pried open the lid. Then he dropped both ends of the tube into the bin and began shaking it frantically. Something deep within him, a primeval blood lust, compelled him forward. Harder and harder he shook the tube. Eventually the squirrel thumped out, landing on a bed of leaf litter at the bottom of the bin. Helpless and quivering, it looked up at Max in a way that seemed imploring. But Max was unfazed; he had become numb to violence. Without thinking twice he retrieved the gun and shot the squirrel pointblank. It squirmed, then went limp and oozed down through a gap in the leaves. Max closed the bin, stepped back, and looked triumphantly out over the neighborhood, the common areas a seeming wasteland of rotting squirrel carcasses.

The sudden absence of ground squirrels did not go unnoticed. The next afternoon Mrs. Parks accosted Max as he was about to pull his car into his garage. Reluctantly, he stopped and put down the driver's side window.

She shuffled toward the car, her flip-flops slapping the soles of her feet with each hurried step. Leaning through the open window, inches from his face, she said breathlessly, "You have to *do* something."

He drew away from her. "Do something about what?"

"About the rat," she said. She looked in the direction of a furry lump lying near the Sandbergs' driveway. Her dog Freddie, it seemed, had found a dead rat on the street and had eaten part of it before she could prevent him. "It's the biggest, most god-awful rat I've ever seen, and I don't have the stomach to clean it up myself. Would you mind doing it?" She gave Max a knowing look. "You seem to be good at that kind of thing."

He told her he would, both out of curiosity and to get rid of her. But what he found after they parted was not a rat. It was one of the ground squirrels he had shot the previous day. Freddie must have dragged it from between the water-meter plates. Max understood why Mrs. Parks did not have the stomach to remove it, as he hardly did himself. Out in the open the smell was only faintly putrid, like a piece of meat in the early stages of decay, but the state of the squirrel's corpse was nothing short of grotesque. The sun had bloated it to nearly twice its original size, and Max could have sworn, when he knelt down to get a better look, that he saw something move near its tail. *Maggots of a house fly? Could they really propagate overnight?* Luckily, it was garbage pick-up day and the Sandbergs' garbage bin was nearby. He retrieved a shovel, scooped up the gaseous monstrosity with a modicum of effort, and dropped it into the bin. That was the last, he hoped, he would have to deal with ground squirrels for a while.

* * *

As it turned out, it *was* the last he had to deal with ground squirrels; it just was not the last he had to deal with rodents. A vacuum had been created by the decimation of the squirrels, and something more pernicious began to take their place. Three weeks after the incident with Freddie, Mrs. Parks came running to Max's front door early in the morning. She was still wearing her nightdress. Her hair was disheveled, and she had dark patches under her eyes as if she were sleep deprived. "Rats again," she said, nearly hyperventilating. He had not told her that the "rat" Freddie found had actually been a squirrel; it would have raised uncomfortable questions. "I think they've gnawed through the engine of my car," she continued. "I can't get it started. And I found bits of wire and hose on the ground by the front tires."

By rats he presumed she meant packrats. To him they were not quite as nasty as brown rats, which roamed the sewers. Packrats seemed more hygienic because they nested in woodpiles or under the thorny protection of prickly pear. Even so, he despised them. He saw one, once, at the crack of dawn while he was on a walk. It came creeping out of a drainage pipe, its long, furry tail trailing disgustingly behind it. His stomach churned at the thought. The last thing he wanted was an animal like that sneaking around his garage. "I'll do what I can," he said, deliberately tempering his enthusiasm, since he knew combating packrats would not be easy.

They were a tricky bunch, for sure. Unlike ground squirrels, rats were nocturnal, and wilier. You could not shoot them, and they could easily outsmart the average trap. Poison was probably the best route. A little cyanide, perhaps. Or an anticoagulant. He was aware of one under the chemical name brodifacoum, a rodenticide that apparently worked wonders by making the animals bleed to death internally. Not a happy thought, but then, what was the alternative? Something worse, that was what. Already Max knew what he would do: strategically place around the neighborhood peanut-butter crackers laced with Rodenthor—although before he could proceed, he would have to convince Eileen and the neighbors of the merits of chemical warfare, which would be a hard sell. Collateral damage and all that. He might be better off going rogue and keeping them in the dark. Either way, he could see that a solution to the problem was a long way off. In fact it appeared the war against rodents had only just begun.

NATHANIEL AND HIS WIFE CAROLINE were driving up Catalina Highway toward Mount Lemmon, which they planned to hike, when the argument he thought they had resolved before leaving the house started all over again.

"I told you we shouldn't have come," Caroline said, looking out the passenger-side window at the patches of white along the highway that were fast becoming sizable snowdrifts. By the time they reached the Palisades Visitor Center, moments later, everything within sight—the gift shop, the ranger's cabin, the surrounding stands of Douglas fir and Arizona and ponderosa pine—was covered in a thick layer of powder. Though it had stopped snowing hours ago, hiking seemed inadvisable now. Caroline had argued as much earlier that morning while grudgingly getting dressed.

"It's just a little snow," Nathaniel said and turned up Sinatra's "White Christmas" that was playing on the car stereo.

She watched his fingers move the dial, in rhythm to the song's words *And may all your Christmases be white.* "You never listen to me," she said under her breath, just loud enough to be heard. Then slowly, abstractedly, she returned her gaze to the wintery landscape outside.

With that, Nathaniel lost his appetite for music. He turned off the stereo, and the two of them drove in silence for the remainder of the journey.

A half-mile from the trailhead, a barrier gate blocked the road. Conditions were too treacherous for vehicles to go any farther. Nathaniel parked the car on the side of the road.

Caroline looked at him questioningly as if to ask "Are we really going through with this?"

He felt her eyes on him but pretended not to notice. "We'll have to hoof it from here," he said, putting on his beanie and getting out of the car.

As he stepped toward the trunk to retrieve his pack, the snow, six inches deep in places, crunched beneath his boots. The air was crisp, and the wind nipping at his face caused him to pull his gaiter up over his mouth and nose. Just above the din of the wind, he could hear a faint trickle of water coming from the creek that ran parallel to the road. He slipped his pack over his shoulders and, looking past the gate in the direction of the trailhead, took in his surroundings. The gorge was a study in white, the browns of the tree trunks and the grays of the rock formations the only elements of contrast. Some of the smaller conifers were covered in so much snow, they bowed under the weight. Here and there sheared branches and downed logs lay in ruins on the forest floor. Overhead, the yellow-white disc of the sun shone brilliantly behind the tops of the tallest trees. Light filtered down through the branches onto the snow below, making it almost blinding to look at. Nathaniel averted his eyes, unzipped the breast pocket of his jacket, pulled out his sunglasses, and put them on. For a brief moment he stared defiantly into the whiteness, at the same time thinking of the challenges the day might offer, how there was nothing under the sun he would not be prepared for.

Caroline had yet to emerge from the car. He went to the passenger-side window and rapped on it. Without waiting for her, he started for the trail. A hundred feet or so down the road, he heard the car door creak open, then slam shut. He pressed the lock button on the key fob and slowed his pace for her to catch up.

"You would have gone without me, wouldn't you?" she said as she came abreast with him, her breath rising in long, vaporous wisps.

He did not answer. Instead, he pointed at the Abert's squirrel that was busying itself at the base of a large pine tree. Its tufted ears and bushy tail made it look more like a fox than a squirrel. Nathaniel lowered his gaiter. "I've never seen one with its winter coat on before," he said, a little louder than was necessary. The sound of his voice sent the squirrel scampering up the slope, leaping from log to log, its tail by turns blending in or contrasting with the snow.

After the squirrel had disappeared, Nathaniel's expression became serious. "Look," he said, gesturing to the ground. "Not a single boot print besides ours. It's just you and me and the animals." There was a tinge of excitement in his voice. "And you know what that means."

"That we're going to die?"

He laughed in spite of himself. "No, it doesn't mean that. It means we'll be the first to break the trail in the snow."

She tucked a loose strand of her bangs into her pom-pom hat and stared intently at the forbidding forest they were about to enter. "That's what I was afraid of."

Another silence fell between them as they made their way down the road to the trailhead, where they arrived fifteen minutes later. Near the signpost was a series of boot prints leading up the trail.

"So much for that," Nathaniel said with disappointment. He

looked toward the other side of the gulch. What seemed to be the tracks of a single hiker meandered down the far slope, over the bridge, and across the parking lot. "They must have come in off the Sunset Trail."

Caroline smirked.

Nathaniel turned and glanced up the steep ascent of the Marshall Gulch Trail and at the imprints of the boots that only a short time before had sunk deeply into the snow. Whoever the person was, he thought, they clearly had gumption to hike alone in this. The thought roused in Nathaniel his competitive spirit; it was a matter of pride for him to do at least as much as the other hiker had done. "Let's go," he said suddenly and with a burst of energy scaled the initial uphill stretch of trail and stomped through the snow—his boots sometimes landing in the existing prints, sometimes not. At the top of the hill, he called over his shoulder, "Are you coming?"

"I'm coming," Caroline said as she plodded forward, one deliberate step at a time.

He did not slow down until the first creek crossing, despite the slick rocks and deepening snow on the trail. The creek followed the contours of a ravine. His impulse upon approaching the water was to get a running start and leap across. But it was deeper and wider than usual, and there was ice at its edges. Twelve feet across might prove too much for him to clear in a single bound. And that was the last thing he needed: to fall into the water and be soaked for the duration of the hike. Besides, if *he* were unable to make the jump, Caroline certainly would not be able to. He would have to wait for her whether he wanted to or not.

Where was she now, anyway? He scanned for a sign of her. Through a narrow gap in the trees a couple hundred yards back he could see the fur pom-pom and eggplant-colored cashmere of her hat moving haltingly on the trail. It was just like her, he thought, to go so slowly. That was why he preferred to hike alone, the way the other hiker had done. But Caroline insisted they spend more time together. She meant dinner or a concert, of course, not a hike. The hike was his idea. He remembered with amusement the look on her face when he first suggested it. She did not enjoy the outdoors like he did. During the five years of their marriage, their differing interests had been a constant bone of contention between them, to the point that they now lived separate, parallel lives. They agreed in principle that something needed to be done about it, but what that might mean in practice neither of them knew, although going on a hike, to Nathaniel's mind, was the perfect first step, a way to rekindle their former fondness and admiration for each other. It was not his fault a severe snow storm hit the mountains only a day before their planned outing.

Maybe she would soften toward him and the hike when she found him waiting to help her across the creek. It did not seem too much to hope for. The act of waiting for her itself should win him some points. But there also would be the literal lending to her of his hand, a romantic gesture if ever there was one. He could see the moment now in his imagination, frozen in time as it were: her last step from a strategically placed stone in the water as she reached for his hand, and him, on the opposite bank, drawing her to safety.

The image faded from Nathaniel's mind, and all that remained was the stark reality of the water, how best to cross it without getting wet. He glanced back toward Caroline. She was coming around a bend, only a stone's throw away from him now. Which reminded him: he needed to test the stability of the stepping stones in the water before she arrived. Already there were two large ones, fully submerged in water, at four-foot intervals between the banks. The other hiker appeared to have used these; their tracks stopped on this side of the creek, then picked up again on the other side. And if the other hiker could do it, Nathaniel was certain he and Caroline could, too.

He leapt without another thought. One foot then the other landed firmly on the first of the stones. He stood there a moment surprised at his own daring, the water lapping his boots. Then cautiously he shifted his weight from side to side. The stone did not move. He stared down at it, at the water swirling around and washing over his boots, and felt a momentary sense of calm.

But even from four feet away he could tell that the second stone would not be so easy. It was not embedded in the creek like the one he was standing on. And it was oddly shaped, almost like an anvil, with more surface area on the top than on the bottom. His foot placement on landing would have to be precise down to the centimeter, only slightly left of center. He readied himself to jump, balancing on his right foot as he swung his left leg like a pendulum.

This time when he landed, the stone moved. He started to fall but instinctively stretched out an arm as a counterweight and, with a nimble movement of his upper torso, gained equilibrium on the stone, only to nearly fall again at the sound of laughter.

"You looked like a gymnast righting yourself on a balance beam," Caroline said with mirth from the bank behind him.

He was not amused. "We'll see who's laughing when it's your turn." Keeping his head and eyes straight to the front, he gently rocked back and forth until the stone beneath his feet settled more firmly into the creek bed. Only then did he jump. He cleared the edge of the water by a foot and landed dead center in one of the boot prints of the other hiker. A self-satisfied smirk formed on his lips as he stepped forward. He was determined to taunt Caroline in her own attempt to traverse the creek. But when he turned around, she was already safely ensconced on the second stone.

"I bet you weren't expecting that, were you?" she said, and leapt before he could position himself to help her. Her foot came down on the bank only an inch or two from the water. She was falling backward, her arms cruciform, as he reached for her. His fingers brushed against the nylon of her jacket, but that was all. She hit the water with a splash, and afterward just sat there, her legs spread-eagled, leaning back on her hands and staring sullenly into her lap, wet and miserable-looking.

"I won't say a word," Nathaniel said, exquisitely aware of the irony. He leaned forward, took her by the hand, and pulled her to her feet.

Not once, even as their hands touched, did Caroline look at him. She stood on the bank now staring vacantly in the direction of the trailhead. Water dripped from her gloves and pants and made teardrop-sized perforations in the snow.

"Do you want to turn back?"

She shook her head. "Just give me a minute," she said, sounding both wounded and contrite. Finally she looked at him. "Actually, you don't have to wait for me if you don't want to."

"I'll wait." He watched her as she removed her waterlogged gloves and swatted them, one at a time, against her thigh.

"Now they're just a *teeny bit* soggy," she said and made a face as she pulled the gloves back on.

Nathaniel's enthusiasm dampened, too, after that. As soon as he resumed the hike, with Caroline again bringing up the rear, he found himself going painfully slowly. There was another creek crossing a short distance ahead, and he did not want her to have any more mishaps if he could help it.

She groaned upon seeing the water.

"It's not nearly as bad as the other one," he said, trying to encourage her. "In fact it's so shallow we could walk through it."

"I'm not walking through it. My boots are wet enough as it is."

"How about I carry you across?"

"Don't be silly."

"I'm serious." He knelt down in front of the water for her to climb onto his back.

She remained where she was.

"What are you waiting for?"

"You might fall. Then we'll both be wet."

"I won't fall."

"But what if you do?" Even as she asked the question she must have gotten over her qualms because she climbed onto his back.

With a grunt he raised himself to his feet, and she wrapped her legs around his waist and tightened her grasp around his neck. In a matter of seconds they were through the water and on the opposite bank.

"See," Nathaniel said, eyeing Caroline over his shoulder.

She giggled and kissed him on the cheek, then lowered her feet to the ground and let go of his neck.

"Wasn't that fun? Doesn't being here"—he motioned to the forest around them, took a deep breath of the fresh, cold air—"make you feel alive?"

In the silence that followed, their eyes were simultaneously drawn to a small waterfall that was flowing onto an accumulation of rocks nearby. The water at the base of the fall spattered and swirled and made soft gurgling noises.

"It's lovely," Caroline said.

"That's precisely—" Nathaniel started to say. But nature, it occurred to him, did not need his advocacy; it could speak for itself.

Back on the trail, as other parts of the forest demanded their attention, the communion between them ended. Just past the rain gauges, where the trees thinned out and the terrain steepened, the snow became deeper so that Caroline sank up to her shins with every step. The trail also became harder to find. At the first of a series of switchbacks, Nathaniel lost sight of the other hiker's tracks and veered off in the wrong direction into a two-foot snowdrift. He stopped and looked around uncertainly, his legs encased in snow. He had been on this hike many times before but never in winter, and none of the landmarks seemed familiar now that they were blanketed in white.

"Please don't tell me we're lost!" Caroline cried, twenty yards behind him, her own legs encased in snow.

He refused to dignify her comment with a response, annoyed that she would even suggest such a thing. But in actuality all he knew for sure was that they were going west. As for the trail—well, that was another matter.

The sun suddenly vanished behind a veil of whitish clouds. Its luminous halo sat just above a stand of trees to the east. Something about the orientation and quality of the refracted light in the sky, how it distorted and made spectral the charred remains of the pine snags along the trail, gave Nathaniel a clue as to their whereabouts. He squinted obliquely up the hill to the southeast, caught a glimpse of one of the other hiker's tracks.

"It's this way," he said, turning and looking back as he began to slog through the snow again.

Caroline, however, stayed rooted to her spot. She shielded her eyes with a hand and surveyed what lay ahead: the hill; the snow; the living trees, and the dead—all of it, her body language seemed to say, without end. "How much further is it?" she asked.

"We're almost to the halfway point." He came to a stop when he saw her countenance fall. "You can't quit now," he said. "Not after we've come so far. Not after you survived the creek."

"But I didn't survive it." She pointed at her boots. "Water's soaked through to my socks. I can feel them squish when I walk."

He could not argue with that. Part of him, too, was only going through the motions in encouraging her to continue. It seemed to him that as a hiking partner, she was little more than deadweight, their mutual enjoyment of the waterfall notwithstanding. Who was he trying to kid, anyway, in bringing her up to Mount Lemmon? It would be better for him to cut loose and hike alone. The trail would take half the time to complete without her. "You're sure you'll be okay going back on your own?"

"I'm sure."

"Even across the creek?" As he said this, he envisioned her spread-eagled in the water again, whimpering pathetically and staring into her lap, nothing around for miles save the flora and fauna of the forest.

"I'll manage." She did not utter the words, but he could hear them in her voice, "I can't possibly get any wetter than I am now, can I?"

"Suit yourself," he said and headed toward her, panting as he laboriously plowed through the snow. Once he reached her, he lifted his pack from his shoulders, rummaged through the front pouch, and handed her the car keys, a granola bar, and her water bottle. "That should sustain you till I get back."

She shot a quick glance up the slope he was about to climb. He had turned, before she could speak, and was retracing his steps. "I should be asking if *you'll* be okay," she called after him.

"Now who's being silly? I could do this hike in my sleep." As he rounded the elbow of the switchback, he turned just long enough to see her stare at him, then shrug and go her separate way.

A minute later he was on the crest of the hill, taking a swig from his water bottle and looking back down the trail. A chill breeze was blowing. He removed his beanie and wiped the sweat from his forehead and let the breeze sweep refreshingly across his face and through his hair. Caroline was as far as the rain gauges now. He watched her stumble through the snow and slowly recede into the trees. At her current rate, he mused, she would take another hour to reach the car. He wondered if he could finish the hike in time to beat her there. Under normal circumstances, he would have said yes, but not with the snow getting deeper and deeper the farther he went.

Soon he was at Marshall Saddle, the halfway point of the hike, and discovered to his chagrin that conditions on the trail were indeed getting worse. The resting logs were buried under three feet of snow. A biting wind spiked with ice crystals stung his face, forcing him to pull up his gaiter again. He had planned to stop at the logs and eat an apple and a granola bar, but it was too cold for that. He trudged past the logs to where the Marshall Gulch Trail ended and the Aspen Trail began and looked out along the ridgeline. One snowdrift after another—some of them as high as five or six feet at the base of mature trees—lined the length of the trail for as far as the eye could see. The sight made him think twice. Maybe his decision to continue the hike had been unwise, after all. It was not too late to turn back, and if he were to, Caroline would be the last person to hold it against him. In fact, she would probably be glad of it, a sign, even if only in her mind, that he was thinking of her instead of himself.

But really, at the moment, the only person who mattered to him, besides himself, was the other hiker. Nathaniel could not let himself be one-upped. He had his pride to consider. And at the end of the day, if he were to give up on the hike, it would be his pride, not Caroline, he would have to face.

A sudden gust of wind lashed his body. He gave a start. The other hiker—where had they gone? Their tracks were nowhere to be seen. Maybe they had chickened out. Then Nathaniel remembered: he had been so distracted by the wind and snow upon arriving at the saddle, he did not register the significance of the tracks that were heading northeast on the far side of the resting logs. The other hiker went the easy way back.

Nathaniel smiled to himself and set off on the Aspen Trail. Beyond the cover of trees, the snow was never less than two feet deep. But even among the trees, going mostly uphill, his progress remained slow. He thought he had passed the worst of it when he came to a clearing that fronted an enormous stand of locust and pine. Hidden beneath the windswept snowbanks, the features of the clearing were unrecognizable. He went one way when he should have gone another and slipped on a patch of ice.

Before he knew what was happening, he was glissading down a hill. He whisked past a pine sapling and clutched at a branch. For a split second he caught hold of it. His body torqued, slamming him onto his stomach and knocking the wind out of him. But still he kept sliding. Wildly he dug striations with his fingers into the icy snow. He skidded for another thirty feet, until he jounced over an outcropping of rock and came to an abrupt halt. His heart was pounding so violently, he could hardly breathe. He rolled onto his back and just lay there, unable to think, aware only of a generalized ache in his lower extremities, staring at the sky and trying to catch his breath.

Finally he sat up, and saw that the soles of his boots were only inches away from a precipice. He jerked back onto his hands and frantically crab-crawled up the slope. The snow he kicked up in the process cascaded over the cliff and into the canyon below.

His heart was still racing even after he had made his way back to the trail. He replayed in his mind over and over again his slide down the hill and his subsequent narrow escape. Did that really just happen? Did he really almost die? A thrill went through him at the thought.

Now his trek through the snowdrifts in the clearing seemed easy and prosaic compared to his brush with death. He was mildly disappointed as he re-entered the cover of trees and the wind died down and the snow lessened. But the moment he emerged from the trees, ascending a steep incline, the forest opened up again, and his disappointment turned into vexation instead of joy. He could feel his body sway as he leaned into the wind and followed the trail's sinuous course for the next mile. Step after arduous step, snow wedged up under the hems of his pants, melted, and seeped into his boots.

Still, he pushed on. At one point, after briefly getting lost, he came up over a hill and realized he had reached the southernmost part of the trail, before it turned east and descended downhill into an aspen grove. He was finally on the homestretch. Without stopping, he drew forward his glove from the face of his watch and checked the time. It was eleven o'clock. Caroline was probably back to the car by now. He did not want to keep her waiting for too long; he would never live it down if he were to. He estimated conservatively that the hike would take him another forty-five minutes to complete. If he quickened his pace, though, he might be able shave off five or ten minutes from that.

But going downhill was no easier. The elbows of the switchbacks were icy, and each time he encountered one, he had to slow down and carefully navigate the edges of the trail. It was causing him to lose time. He knew he would have to speed up, or he would be lucky to reach the car by noon. At last he got to the point where the intervals between the switchbacks lengthened and the trail more or less straightened out. His stride lengthened in turn. Shortly he was in the aspen grove, surrounded by the papery white bark of the trees, approaching the last of the switchbacks. At its elbow, he threw caution to the wind and practically flung himself down the slope.

He went into freefall for what seemed like an eternity, and hit the tree well with such force that something in his body snapped.

A white light flashed and splintered. He felt a burning pain shoot up his spine. Then darkness descended, but not before a strange image took shape in his mind. He was in an aspen grove, moving hauntingly through the trees. All around him was a sea of white: the snow, the scarred bark, the cirrostratus clouds. And though it was dead of winter, still the leaves of the leafless trees, like myriad phantom limbs, quaked and susurrated in the wind.

No one, not a solitary soul, heard him whimper.

The Holiday Blizzard

FROM HIS WINDOW SEAT, David could barely see the wing of the plane, let alone the skies above of Denver, for all the snow that was falling. The storm had struck with such suddenness, he was reminded of the whiteouts he experienced skiing on the slopes of Boulder in his youth. One minute he would be slaloming down a mountain under a clear blue sky, tightly carving the line he had picked; the next, he would be on the verge of a face-plant, the sky and everything else around him shrouded in fog. Once, in his teens, he was on a black-diamond run—the "Cannonball" run, he seemed to recall—when a whiteout hit. Before he could stop and wait for the fog to lift, he caught an edge turning on a mogul and went tumbling down the slope like a rag doll. He managed to escape with only minor injuries, but after his fall, he lay there in the snow for over an hour, disoriented and staring into nothingness, before the ski patrol finally found him.

The plane started to shake. David could hear luggage shifting in the overhead bins. The cup of ice on his tray table slid, hesitated, then slid some more. He caught it midair as it shot off the table toward his lap. In the same instant a ding reverberated through the cabin, and the captain's voice came over the PA system. David wedged the cup between his legs, stowed the tray table, fastened his seatbelt, and then watched the passengers in the aisle scramble unsteadily to their seats.

Curiously, throughout the commotion, the woman seated next to him had not budged. Somehow she remained fast asleep, her head tilted back, snoring. A flurry of negative emotions swept over David as he looked at her now. She could not have been more than fifty, but her mannish features made her seem much older. She had a trace of down on her upper lip, and her voice was deep and husky like a heavy smoker's. Earlier on the flight, she had chatted David up, volunteering her name—Barbara—and telling him about her job—retail buyer—and about all the interesting places to which it regularly took her. He did not want to talk—he had too much on his mind—but it sounded to him like Barbara was living out of a suitcase, and he felt sorry for her. He knew what it was like being a slave to corporate America. His own experiences in the business world had been less than ideal. He confessed to Barbara that his trip to Denver was, in point of fact, a last-ditch effort to save his consulting career. Only weeks before, his boss retired unexpectedly, leaving him in the lurch. And now … David was mid-sentence—about to explain that he was on his way to meet a prospective client in Denver at the law firm Lane & Mather—when Barbara glanced at his ring finger, saw his wedding band, and, nevertheless, gave him a leer. At first he thought he imagined it, but then she asked him what hotel he was staying at and continued the line of questioning from there. Maybe, if he weren't too busy, they could meet up somewhere for dinner? She knew of a great Brazilian restaurant on Northfield Boulevard near his hotel that he might like. At the suggestion, David flushed. *Brazilian*, did she say? Oh, as it happened, he wasn't very fond of Brazilian. The fortuitous arrival of a stewardess offering peanuts and pretzels saved him from further prevarication. He took a bag of each, ate them with the absorption of a man starving to death, and then drifted into a prolonged and decidedly pretend sleep.

Something was rattling on the bulkhead between first class and coach, as if a screw were loose. Between that and Barbara's snoring, David could not hear himself think. And he needed to think. What was he going to do if he missed his client meeting? That was becoming a distinct possibility because of the weather. During the last minute, the visibility through his window had worsened. He could not see even the wing now. Beyond the flecks of frost on the windowpane was a wall of white.

Barbara woke with a start. "What's going on?" she asked in a hoarse whisper. She squinted at the bulkhead. "It sounds like the plane's falling apart."

"A storm," David said. Without looking at her, he gestured toward the window.

"My God, where'd *that* come from?"

"Out of nowhere." At least, that was what he supposed. Before leaving his house for the Phoenix airport, he had not actually checked Denver's weather report. He had lived in the desert for so long, he forgot how disruptive snowfall could be in winter. It seemed unlikely, in any event, that an airline would knowingly send its passengers into the eye of a storm.

The turbulence intensified and all at once the plane dropped several feet.

David felt his stomach lighten. In apparent alarm Barbara leaned into him, her hand brushing against his on the armrest. He made as if to recoil but did not. She appeared to be genuinely frightened. Maybe she was human after all, he thought, and not so different from himself. She might even be in the same boat as he, working in the world of business not because she wanted to but because she had to, because it was expected of her. In fact, it was not too much to suppose that her personality had greater depth than he gave her credit for. And even if she *were* feigning fright, even if her behavior *had been* a puerile attempt to touch him, so what? Clearly she was lonely, and a little human contact never hurt anyone.

Another voice came over the PA system, asking the flight attendants to prepare for landing. The plane shook as it began its descent, and the bulkhead continued to rattle. All the while Barbara sat rigidly in her seat, staring past David into the void outside and mouthing something.

The Lord's Prayer? David wondered. An odd thing to do, if it were. Not to say incongruous. One moment she was making a pass at him; the next she was calling on God.

But then, who was David to judge? No one was above reproach. He had had to learn that himself the hard way. At every turn on his thirteen-year journey as a consultant, people and circumstances had let him down, each new disappointment chipping away at his idealism until all that remained was the raw pulp of cynicism. And he was sick of it. He was sick of thinking ill of people, of life. Why did he always have to be so moralistic about everything? It occurred to him that for every venal megalomaniac he encountered in his business dealings, there were at least a hundred ordinary people just like him— like Barbara?—trying to make a living, and leading lives of quiet despair.

He looked out the window again or at least tried to. He still could not see the wing of the plane, and now the frost crystals spanned the entirety of the window like the feathery tendrils of a fern.

"You must think me silly," Barbara said, her gaze shifting from the window to David. She paused, and he thought she might be easing into an apology. Instead she said, "But I've never gotten used to this. Flying in bad weather, I mean."

No sooner had she spoken than the plane yawed slightly. A

gasp went up from the passengers in chorus.

David made eye contact with Barbara for the first time since she invited him to dinner. "It's enough to unman even the stouthearted," he said. "So no, I don't think you're silly."

She smiled faintly, closed her eyes, and went back to clenching the armrests as if she were in the harrowing grip of a dentist's chair.

If anyone were silly, David thought, *he* was. What was he doing, flying on a plane in the middle of a blizzard, going to a meeting that had only a slim chance of success? And if by some miracle the meeting happened, and he managed to convince Gary Wallick, one of the partners at Lane & Mather, to retain him, then what? He might end up on a path as soul-crushing as the last thirteen years had been.

One saving grace was that he and Gary got on well, and so schmoozing would be less distasteful. They had first met through David's former boss and had hit it off immediately, despite the twenty-year age gap between them. There was something prepossessing about Gary, a high-powered attorney who had not forgotten his roots. He spoke in and out of court with the easy manner of a Heartland native, and his appearance was in keeping with his background. He wore a full beard and looked the part of a true mountain man, even in a suit. He also—and this was the clincher in David's mind—spent every other weekend during the winter months on Eldora Mountain, where David had cut his teeth as a skier.

Really, though, David had little choice in the matter. His company recently gave him an ultimatum: either start generating business of his own, or he could find himself a new employer. So doing business with Gary would be the lesser of two evils, as well as the path of least resistance.

With a sudden bang the plane's wheel wells opened. In the disquiet that followed, all that could be heard was the wind pummeling the fuselage and, in counterpoint to that, the landing gear emitting a steady hydraulic groan.

Barbara's eyes opened. Her face had gone pale.

"We'll be safely on the ground soon," David said to reassure her. He knew enough about planes to know that they were built to withstand even the heaviest of storms. What he did not know, however, was what would happen after the plane landed. He doubted the Denver airport would be equipped to handle this much snow all at once. He could see it already: thousands of people queuing up at airline information desks demanding answers, discovering that they would be stranded for hours, and grudgingly crashing willy-nilly on arrival-gate chairs, airport-supplied cots, or the floor. And because it was only five days before Christmas, the crowds at the airport would be worse than usual. David resolved to avoid being stranded at all costs. Luckily he was traveling lightly, with only a single carry-on, and so he would not have to go to baggage claim. The moment he de-boarded the plane, he could make a beeline for ground transportation. He would do whatever it took, short of pushing people out of the way, to get to his hotel before the day was through. Not even an act of God was going to prevent him from missing tomorrow's meeting with Gary.

"Come hell or ten feet of snow," David thought out loud, forgetting he was not alone.

"I'm sorry?" Barbara said. She did not look reassured.

A hundred meters above ground, the plane crabbed into the wind. Outside, the snow had yet to let up, but the visibility had improved just enough that David could make out the faint outlines of roads surrounding the airport. He could also see, almost perpendicular to his window, runway lights and the flashing lights of service vehicles.

The plane was still angled into the wind even after it began to flare, so when it finally touched down on the icy tarmac, the wheels skidded sideways. A deathly silence fell on the cabin. With an unsettling jerk the plane righted itself on the runway. Then the wing flaps and engine shields went up and the passengers were thrown back into their seats. For several hundred meters the brakes screeched, until at last the plane slowed to a rolling stop, turned, and taxied toward the safety of the arrival gate. Everyone except David clapped upon realizing they were out of harm's way.

David shot Barbara an I-told-you-so look.

She lowered her hands, forced a smile.

In the concourse, he was annoyed to find that his imagination had been lacking. The number of holiday travelers was much greater than he expected. Everywhere he looked, people clogged the walkways, and those who were not standing in line at gates or at shops were just milling about looking confused. It was utter chaos, but David remained focused. He kept a sharp lookout for the subway signs and methodically weaved his way through the crowds.

A constant chattering of voices filled the air. "They can't do this!" David heard someone yell at one point. He turned and saw an outraged traveler gesticulating like a madman in front of an information booth. The behavior seemed disproportionate, but that was before the announcement came on about the airport's immediate closure.

"What the hell?" David said under his breath, descending the escalator to the subway. How could the airport close so soon? His plane had landed barely fifteen minutes ago. Was the storm really that bad? If so, he needed a taxi, and quick.

At the subway station, he took a train to Jeppesen Terminal, where he went to Level 5 and spilled through the electronic doors out into the cold, gusty air. He stood there stunned on the sidewalk for a moment. Apparently he was the only one bold or stupid enough to venture outside, as no other passengers were in sight. Nor were there any vehicles in the taxi and shuttle pick-up lanes. A traffic guard stood on the pedestrian crosswalk near the farthest median. Behind her, beyond the overpass, the snow was coming down furiously. The wind sent flakes of it swirling about her feet.

She waved at him. "There aren't any cabs," she called out above the wind. "I suggest the two of you go back inside."

The *two of you*? David thought. At the same time he felt a bodily presence behind him. He turned. It was Barbara. "Oh," he said, and nearly choked.

"What are we going to do now?" Barbara asked.

"*We*?" he said incredulously. He could abide her inviting him to dinner in a moment of weakness, but to follow him? His pity had its limits.

She let go of the telescopic handle on her bag and took a deep breath. "Boy, do you walk fast. I had a hard time keeping up. Through the concourse, you were like Moses parting the sea." When he failed to respond, she added, "Except it wasn't water you were parting, of course. It was bodies."

"I get it," he said, turning around again. There was still no taxi. But up the road, through the vertical blur of snow, he could see the blue-white light of headlights approaching.

"If you're waiting for a cab," the traffic guard said, "you'll be waiting an awfully long time. No one's crazy enough to drive in this."

The headlights drew nearer. David stepped onto the crosswalk. "I wouldn't be so sure of that," he said.

A few seconds later he was standing on the island for ground transportation when out of the snowy depths a taxi appeared. It pulled up alongside him. The passenger-side window was down.

"Where to?" the driver asked. He wore a parka, a cuffed knit hat, and gloves. He looked less like a cabdriver than an explorer about to embark on a polar expedition.

David poked his head through the open window. "The Mile-High Inn and Suites. Can you get me there?"

"I didn't come all the way out here in nasty-ass weather to go back without a fare. I've got mouths to feed."

"Wait for me!" Barbara hollered and ran across the crosswalk wheeling her bag behind her.

The driver got out of the taxi and stowed David's bag in the trunk. Then, looking from Barbara to David, he asked, "Are you two together?"

"No," David said and intended to leave it at that, but Barbara had already handed the driver her bag.

"I'm going to the Fireside Inn," she said. "You can drop David off first." To David she said cheerfully, "I guess we're sharing a ride."

David averted his eyes. "I guess we are."

"You people are nuts," the traffic guard said as the doors of the taxi opened and closed.

Before he set off, the driver glanced at Barbara and David in the rearview mirror. "You might want to buckle up."

Out in the open, on Peña Boulevard, the visibility was less than twenty feet, but that did little to deter the driver. He maintained a speed of thirty miles an hour and even accelerated a little when the road veered south toward I-70. Meanwhile the windows of the taxi fogged up, even with the defroster on full, and the driver simply lowered his head and peered through the windshield's last remaining patch of clear glass, simultaneously drumming the steering wheel to the alternating beats of the windshield wipers and the Christmas songs on the radio. He seemed to be enjoying himself, and David was beginning to wonder whether the guy *was* nuts. Who in their right mind would drive several miles in whiteout conditions for the sake of a few measly bucks?

As the taxi continued onward, Barbara kept eyeing the back of the driver's head and then looking at David, as if she wanted him to say something. But what could he say? Turning the taxi around was not an option; they were already halfway to their hotels. And then there was the meeting he had in the morning. Given a choice, he would rather risk being buried alive in a wintry grave than give up on his consulting career without a fight.

On I-70, the cabdriver did not decelerate. He did not stop drumming the steering wheel, either, and as a smattering of oncoming traffic began to appear—the headlights emerging now and then like ghosts from another dimension—his drumming grew louder.

The noise seemed to be adding to Barbara's jitters. Suddenly she cried out, "Would you stop that!"

In the time it took the driver to turn his head and snap, "Do want to get to your hotel, lady, or not?" a semitruck from the opposite side of the highway careened through the cement barrier and skidded toward the taxi. The cabdriver swerved and slammed on the brakes. David stuck out his hands to brace himself. Inches from his window he glimpsed the truck's grill and Peterbilt emblem barrel by. Then he and Barbara and the cabdriver lunged forward in their seats as the taxi came to a halt.

"Jesus H. Christ," the cabdriver said, wiping blood from his nose. He eased the taxi onto the shoulder. "You okay back there?"

David's left shoulder was sore, but otherwise he was fine. He looked at Barbara. Her eyes were closed, and she was not moving. The expression on her face was cadaverous. He shook her. "Barbara?"

She opened her eyes slowly, as if waking from the dead. "Have we died and gone to hell?" she asked, seemingly in earnest.

David removed his hand. "We're okay," he said to the driver.

"I need a cigarette," said Barbara, breathing heavily.

"Fucking flatlanders," the driver cursed. "They don't know how to drive." He lifted up the hood of his parka and tightened its drawstrings so that he looked like an Eskimo.

David turned in his seat. The rear window was completely fogged up. "Should we go check on the truck driver? He may not have fared as well as we did."

The cabdriver sneered. "You want to walk around in this weather? On the highway? And for the sake of some dumbfuck? I don't think so." He put the taxi in drive and peeled out onto I-70.

Within a few miles, they were exiting onto Central Park Boulevard, near David's hotel. Its stone-and-brick façade was visible from the street. The cars in the parking lot were covered in several inches of snow. Some of the room lights were on. David found it comforting to know that he would not be the only one waiting out the storm in a hotel. Even more comforting was the fact that he had avoided being stranded at the airport.

The taxi pulled up in front of the hotel. The driver retrieved David's bag, and David paid the fare, to which he added an extra twenty. "I can't say it was a smooth ride," he said, "but you did get me here like you promised."

"Merry Christmas," the driver said, looking a little crazed, his face shadowy beneath his hood and a smear of blood above his lip.

As the taxi drove away, Barbara lowered her window and waved goodbye. "Good luck with your meeting, David! And enjoy the holidays!" Then she and the taxi were swallowed up by the snow.

In the hotel, David checked in at the front desk and took the elevator up to his fifth-floor room. The first thing he did was call 911. He could not stop thinking about the truck driver out there on the highway. Dumbfuck or not, he might need help. After David spoke with the emergency call-taker, he called his wife. The phone rang several times before she answered. When she finally did, she was out of breath as if she had run across the house. She had been worried to death, she said. The Denver storm was all over the news. Was he okay?

He rubbed his shoulder. "I don't even know where to begin."

During the night he had trouble sleeping. He was worried about his meeting, and his shoulder ached. He had taken some painkillers, but they did not work. And the prospect of not being able to meet with Gary only aggravated the pain.

Around one a.m. he got out of bed and drew back the curtains. The snow was falling as heavily as ever. The cars in the parking lot had all but disappeared; in the dim lamplight they were just a series of undulating mounds. If he had not had other things on his mind he would have found this exhilarating, his first white Christmas in years. But his future hung in the balance, and the snow made him feel hemmed in.

He wondered why Denver was so unprepared for the storm. There was a time in his own life when this kind of weather would have been commonplace. In the Boulder of his youth, blizzards were a nuisance but rarely brought life to a standstill. Sometimes schools would not even close. When he was a boy, his mother would bundle him up in snow boots and a snowsuit and send him out in winter squalls to trudge a mile or more to school. No one ever thought twice about it. He remembered when he was in third grade. He had a paper route, and every morning he would deliver the papers come snow, rain, or shine. On the day he was thinking of, a blizzard struck the night before. There were ten-foot snowdrifts in places. Some of the customers on his route had shoveled their sidewalks but most had not. It did not matter. David wrapped the papers in plastic bags and delivered every last one of them, at times having to struggle through snow that went up to his waist. That was over twenty-five years ago. A lot had changed since then—he had gone to college, gotten married, moved to the desert—but in many ways he was still the same person he had always been. He carried into adulthood the same dogged determination, as well as the same intolerance of weakness and ineptitude, in himself no less than in others.

He went back to bed, leaving the curtains open, as if doing so would allow him to breath more freely and at the same time keep the snow in check. The thoughts of his childhood had eased his mind. His shoulder hurt less, too. He fell asleep with the conviction that it would be better to try and fail than to never try at all.

By sunrise the snow had stopped. Outside his room window, a mantle of white stretched toward the horizon. He turned on the TV to one of the local news channels. Throughout the Rocky Mountain Front Range, two to three feet of snow had fallen. Closures were rife. Besides the Denver airport, the city of Denver itself had been shut down, along with interstate highways 25, 76, and 70 and U.S. Routes 36 and 85. The U.S. mail was undeliverable. A statewide disaster had been declared.

"You've got to be kidding me," David muttered to himself. He turned off the TV and tossed the remote onto the bed. What was he going to do now? He was at the mercy of the Denver authorities, who had wussed out before even attempting snow removal. He took out his cell phone and texted Gary. *I'm holed up in my hotel. We'll have to reschedule. Any chance we could meet once the roads are clear?*

While David waited to hear back, he called the airline he flew in on, but the expected wait time for a representative was fifty minutes, so he hung up. Then he called the airport. He got a recorded message saying that the airport was closed and would not be open again for at least twenty-four hours and that passengers should call airlines directly if they had any questions about canceled flights or re-bookings. David expected no less. He was fairly certain that if he were to wait the fifty minutes to talk to an airline representative, he would experience a similar runaround. The representative would tell him, no doubt, to contact the airport, because the airline could not possibly deal with stranded passengers until the airport re-opened. And the ritual passing of the buck would go on and on.

So it did. Later that morning, David went down to the hotel's dining room to find an empty food bar. Breakfast consisted of cornflakes and some day-old bagels and donuts, displayed pathetically on a side table. According to the hotel manager, who had shown up to apologize for the "meager repast"—the man actually used that phrase, to David's annoyance—the food delivery truck could not make it through the snow. It was the city's fault, the manager complained, for not clearing the roads. Because of it, everyone, from one end of Denver to the other, was suffering deprivations. For his part, the manager had had to stay overnight at the hotel without a change of clothes. He showered this morning, but he could not get the stink off. When David asked if the hotel shuttle would be running any time soon—because he, too, needed a change of clothes—the manager laughed derisively. Had David been listening? The roads were impassable. And, anyway, what was the point? It was doubtful any businesses would even be open. The hotel itself was open only because it had to be.

David had a chastened look on his face as the manager left. He sat alone at a table and ate a couple of cake donuts that had the shape and texture of hockey pucks and washed them down with a mug of acrid coffee. A *meager repast*. Inedible crap, more like it. Already he could feel the heartburn coming on.

He checked his cell phone. There was still no word from Gary, but then it was only eight o'clock, and Gary probably had more pressing things to contend with, like digging out his driveway. He, David, would just have to wait.

But that was easier said than done because the day dragged on interminably. Back in his room, he spent several hours watching TV and reading online newspapers, taking breaks only for lunch and dinner, which were almost as bad as the breakfast. Nothing seemed to be going his way. For reasons he could not fathom, by evening the roads still had not been cleared and, worse, Gary still had not responded to his text. And then his head was hurting from staring at screens all day and his stomach was feeling queasy from the stale leftovers he had been forced to eat and the ache in his shoulder had come back and all the sitting and lying around were causing him to go stir crazy, absolutely stir crazy.

His cell phone pinged. He jumped off the bed, grabbed the phone. There was a message from Gary. *Sorry for the late response*, the message read. *It's been a crazy couple of days.* [You don't know the half of it, David thought.] *Roads should be clear by tomorrow. Let's plan to meet in the evening. Will send a follow-up text to firm up details.*

David sat on the edge of the bed. A weight, he felt, had been lifted. He looked out the window. The snowscape had not changed—in the light of the haloed streetlamps, the roads and sidewalks and buildings and trees were still an endless white— but the moon and stars in the sky were more luminous. He had the impulse to do something spontaneous, something an unjaded child might do, something he himself had not done in over fifteen years. He put on his shoes and his barn jacket and headed for the door.

The next thing he knew he was outside, stumbling through the snow. The wind had picked up. He reached down and scooped up two fistfuls of powdery white. Expertly he compacted it, rolled it, compacted it some more, until his bare hands were numb. Then he cocked his arm and chucked the ball as far as he could into the mysterious swirling night.

In the morning he was assailed by a mix of good and bad news. The city's snowplows were finally making progress, but Central Park Boulevard and some of the other arterial roads would not be cleared until midday. For several hours more, he would be stuck in his dirty clothes. The airport, too, was expected to be open by midday, but flights were so backed up, a return flight to Phoenix would not be available for another day and a half. He called his airline and haggled for nearly an hour, only to be given a seat on a red-eye that would get him home in the early hours of Christmas Eve. Yet another of his days would be wasted languishing in a hotel. As for his meeting with Gary, it was rescheduled for five o'clock that evening at the offices of Lane & Mather. But Gary's follow-up message included a qualifier about the meeting's being contingent upon the duration of a deposition he had to take. The implication was that if the deposition went beyond five, the meeting would be canceled and David would be out of luck.

Upon reading Gary's message, David only skimmed the last sentence or two, something about the holidays and the future. Probably no irony had been intended, but that was the way David took it. The future? He did not want to think about the future. There were too many variables to consider, too many unknowns. One thing was certain: if the meeting were canceled, he might not have a future. His consulting work had been so specialized, and he had been doing it for so long, he was not qualified for much of anything else. And even assuming he could transition to another career, he hated the thought of starting over.

The incessant thinking, he knew, was part of his problem. He needed to get his mind off things, to find a diversion. Once the roads were clear, he took a shuttle to a nearby shopping mall. He had a few hours to kill before his meeting, so after he bought some clothes at a department store, he went to a matinee showing of *Nunatak*, a post-apocalyptic movie set in Greenland during the throes of an ice age. Counterproductively it got him thinking again. He came away wondering what would have happened if the recent blizzard had lasted not a day but a week or even a month. Would the world have been able to adapt to such an onslaught? Would *he* have?

Walking back to catch a shuttle, he was so absorbed in his thoughts, he almost failed to notice the holiday lights that had come on. They were everywhere—suspended above the plaza, on store fronts, lamp poles, trees—and they were all the colors of the rainbow. He stopped and looked around. The sun had just dropped behind a row of shops, and in the gray light the decorations were an intimation of the festivities to come. And they *would* come, he thought. Despite the blizzard, life would go on. It *was* going on, all around him. People along the plaza were in good spirits, smiling and chatting—happy, it seemed, to be free from the confines of their homes. But there was something else in their faces—a harried but resilient look—as though they had been beaten down by a trying experience but were stronger for it. Stopping and glancing into a shop window, David saw reflected in the glass a similar look on his own face.

* * *

Lane & Mather was located in a skyscraper downtown. The firm took up the entirety of the forty-third floor. When David arrived at a quarter to five, the receptionist at the front desk led him to a glassed-in conference room that overlooked the city. The Rockies rose up in the distance. A violet streak suffused the skyline; in the sun's afterglow, the snow on the mountains gave off, like a mirage, the shimmery appearance of ice sheets.

David took in the view and then helped himself to a glass of water on a pushcart, after which he went to one of the thirty-odd vacant chairs that surrounded the conference table. The chair swiveled as he sat down, and this struck him as funny. He looked through the glass wall out into the hallway and, seeing that no one was there, pushed his chair back from the table and did a couple of half-turns in each direction. Then, using the table for leverage, he spun the chair as hard as he could.

He was on his second rotation when a man appeared in the doorway. "Am I interrupting something?" the man asked.

David thrust a hand out and clasped the table, abruptly stopping the chair. He stood up.

"You looked like you were having fun," the man said, in a way that suggested fun was not something he had very often.

David suppressed a laugh. "Sorry, I wasn't sure how long I'd be waiting, and—"

"That's why I'm here. My boss, Gary Wallick, sent me."

David recognized the man's voice then. He was the first-year associate with whom David had spoken over the phone two weeks earlier in making arrangements for his trip to Denver. "Are you Christopher Burns?"

"In the flesh."

David went around the table and shook Christopher's hand. "Good to meet you."

"Likewise." Christopher hesitated. Then he said quietly, "I have some bad news, I'm afraid."

David did not need to hear any more. "Gary's not coming."

"He really wanted to, and up until half an hour ago, he thought he would be, but now opposing counsel is insisting the deposition go on for a full seven hours, even though it started late and both parties agreed beforehand it would end at five. Gary doesn't want to keep you waiting. He sends you his best, and asked me to give you this." Christopher handed David a plastic card.

David stared at the thing in his hand. Why did he feel like he had just been given a cheap consolation prize?

"It's to Confluence Bar & Grill, a block from here on Restaurant Row."

Without responding, David pocketed the gift card.

"When's your flight back to Phoenix?"

"Tomorrow night."

"Have a safe trip."

"Yeah," David said. "Thanks."

"Let me escort you out."

They walked silently down a couple of hallways to the front desk, where they tarried a moment and shook hands again.

"Until next time," Christopher said.

"Until next time," David repeated. On his way down the elevator, as he mechanically watched the floor numbers count backwards on the digital display, the only thought going through his mind was that it would be a cold day in hell before there would ever be a "next time."

The elevator reached the first floor and he hurried to the exit and flung open the door onto Lincoln Street. Outside, the air was crisp. Lifting his jacket collar and putting his hands into his pockets, he made his way toward Restaurant Row. Christmas and Hanukkah lights were on display in storefronts and around tree trunks along the street. Despite his glum mood, he could not help being infected by the holiday spirit. He smiled at people as they went by, and some of them deigned to smile back.

Out front of the Confluence Bar & Grill, the menu was posted. He stopped to check it out. The food was a fusion of Asian and European, a confluence of East and West. As he entered the foyer, a hostess informed him of the hour-long wait for a table. Would he prefer to avoid the wait and sit at the bar instead? He said he would.

Five minutes later he was on a barstool, waiting for his food and sipping a beer, when a husky voice, the last one on earth he wanted to hear, came from behind him, "Well, I'll be."

He flinched.

"David! How are you?" She pulled up a stool next to him. He could smell alcohol on her breath.

"Not too bad, all things considered." He faked a smile, did not ask her how *she* was doing.

"How'd your meeting go?"

"Swimmingly."

"Really?"

"Yep."

"How wonderful," she said. "And what about a flight back to Phoenix? Did you find one that leaves before Christmas?"

"I did. Tomorrow night at 11:30."

"Oh my gosh. That's the same flight I'm on."

"You don't say." He was beyond incredulity now.

"Maybe we'll be seated next to each other again."

"Maybe," he said. "That would be quite the cap to my trip."

His food arrived. He had no desire to eat with her watching him, so he offered to buy her dinner. The irony was not lost on him, but he thought it might be nice to have someone to talk to while he ate, to have a familiar face around, even if it was hers.

She thanked him but declined his offer. She had already eaten, she said, and had just concluded a client meeting as David was entering the restaurant. "You can buy me a drink, though."

"All right. What'll you have?"

"The same thing you're having."

He placed the order. Feeling generous, he retrieved the gift card from his pocket. "Compliments of Lane & Mather," he said, as the bartender set Barbara's beer in front of her. "Before I go hog wild and buy a drink for everyone at the bar, I should find out how much is on this." He handed the bartender the card, who scanned it into the register.

"Ten bucks," the bartender said.

David thought he misheard. "Say that again?"

"Ten bucks."

He stared disbelievingly at the bartender. *Ten bucks*? That was par for the course. His trip to Denver, when all was said and done, was going to cost him over $1,000—plane ticket, hotel, food, cabs, new clothes—and four days of his life, and all Gary could do was give him a gift card worth half an entrée? "Frickin' cheapskate."

"Who?" Barbara asked.

"No one," David said, trying to end the conversation before it began.

She leaned toward him. "It's okay," she said. "You can tell me." As she spoke, he noticed a bit of foam on her moustache. He signaled to her by running a finger along his upper lip, but she did not pick up on it.

Smiling, he turned to his food. He was famished all of a sudden. Before he could swallow his first bite, Barbara launched into a story about the hardships she had endured during the past two days, but he was not listening. On the wall behind the bar was a TV, and the five-thirty news had come on. The first segment was about the Breckenridge Ski Resort, how spectacular the skiing conditions were in the aftermath of the blizzard. As the images of the pristine runs flitted across the screen, David felt a quiver of nostalgia. Ever since he moved to Phoenix, he had gone skiing only a handful of times, twice in Boulder while visiting family and three times at Arizona Snowbowl. Maybe that was what he could do with his future, at least in the short run: take some time off and spend a winter skiing. In his mind he was already back on Eldora Mountain, breaking in the more challenging trails like he did as a teenager, back when his whole life stretched out before him. He wondered, if he had known then where his life would lead him, whether he would have done things differently. He did not doubt that he would have. But to believe that his future was unalterable because of his past implied that his current life, at the age of thirty-five, had reached a sort of runout, when in reality there was an entire course line to follow before it would end. He had time enough yet to do something meaningful with his life.

Like Flesh to the Scalpel

OR AS LONG AS I CAN REMEMBER, my conception of the nervous breakdown has been of a condition at once repugnant and romantic: repugnant in the sense that revealing such human frailty is weak and unattractive; romantic because it suggests, to the literary-minded at least, an artistic temperament. I am admittedly stoical by nature, thanks to my German ancestry, so I generally find off-putting any excessive show of emotion or anxiety. Despite this, I have never been able to fully dissociate the idea of a nervous breakdown from certain alluring stories of artists or literary figures. Among others, Van Gogh and Sherwood Anderson come to mind. I have these recurring images. One is of Van Gogh in Arles, screaming at Gauguin that he has outstayed his welcome, a razor in his trembling and bloodied hand, a part of his severed left ear incongruously amid charcoal sketches strewn on the floor of his house on the Place Lamartine. Another image is of Sherwood Anderson sitting in his wainscoted office of the Anderson Manufacturing Co. in Elyria, Ohio. His head is buried in his hands, and he is cringing at the thought of the day's mind-numbing work ahead of him, of being called the "roof-fix man" for the umpteenth time. He is determined, once and for all, to throw it all up and escape from his unbearable materialistic existence.

These are just my imaginings, as I said. Reality is rarely so tantalizing. In fact, it is usually much more mundane and sometimes even borders on the repulsive, as was the case with my own breakdown. Try as I might in hindsight, I see little romance in the days that led up to what my family now embarrassingly refers to as my period of temporary insanity. I did not, for example, let my hair grow out or start wearing brightly colored strips of cloth in place of neckties, as Anderson is said to have done during *his* breakdown.

So where do I begin? The breakdown itself occurred recently, but to do justice to my story, I should begin over ten years ago when I was a young Marine working in a military-intelligence installation up the road from the Pentagon. I look back on those days with a mixture of nostalgia and regret. I enlisted in the Marine Corps at the age of seventeen to escape from what I thought would be a futureless life in my home state of Kansas. My first several months in the military were miserable. It was like being trapped in a nightmarish Orwellian dystopia. I think I can honestly say without exaggerating that my experiences in boot camp caused me to lose my religion. With time, however, I adjusted to the life of deprivation and discipline, and at my first duty station in Arlington, Virginia, I was quickly promoted to corporal and even grew to enjoy the relative freedom and intrigue that working night shifts in a Marine-intelligence unit afforded me. Each shift lasted twelve hours, but because usually there would be only an hour or two of work during any given shift, I and my colleagues would sleep or play video games or listen to music to while away the time. Then we would spend the better part of our days sightseeing, hanging out at the mall, or playing golf. Excepting the physical rigor of which every Marine was required to partake, my last two years in the Marine Corps were basically one continuous vacation.

All this came to a crashing halt one day about nine months before my four-year tour of duty was scheduled to end. I had just come off a shift, and my unit was on a long-distance run that took us along the Potomac, across the Arlington Memorial Bridge and past the Lincoln Memorial, through some of the nicer parts of Northwest D.C., and back down the south side of Fort Meyer. I was a good runner, and I and one or two of the others in my unit often led the pack on our compulsory runs. That day was no different. By the time we reached the final leg of our run, I was a half-mile or more ahead of everyone else. I remember feeling tired but invigorated. Few things are as satisfying as a runner's high. As I veered north onto Columbia Pike toward Southgate Road, I slowed my pace a bit to let the others catch up. If I had learned anything during my time in the Marine Corps, it was that it would be highly inappropriate to outrun the officers and senior enlisted in my unit. The purpose of our intense physical training was more than just to maintain conditioning and discipline on the off chance of war; it was also intended to be a form of punishment. So to find pleasure in the runs, as I did, was anathema. It was like telling off my superiors to their faces. As it turned out, there was no need for me to consciously slow my pace, because at the very moment the PX and barracks of Headquarters Marine Corps came into view, a jolt of pain shot through my lower extremities. I was forced to pull off the sidewalk and stop. My ankles felt like they were about to give out. I stood there doubled over when some of the other Marines—including Staff Sergeant Stoke, the second-most senior enlisted man in my unit—caught up with me.

"You okay, Mauer?" Stoke asked, jogging in place as he awaited my response, no doubt more concerned about properly warming down than about my health.

"Yeah, I'm okay," I said, and grimaced. This was clearly no run-of-the-mill injury, but I was young and stupid, and I had been conditioned to view any visible show of pain as a sign of weakness. I took a deep breath and jogged the remaining block, past the MPs at the checkpoint and onto base. I figured all I needed was to rest and the pain would subside on its own. After showering, I spent the rest of the day in bed, expecting I would feel better by the time my night shift rolled around. But later that afternoon I awoke from a nap to find that the pain in my ankles was worse, to the point that I could hardly walk.

I barely endured the days and weeks that followed, limiting my movements to the places I couldn't avoid: mostly my office and the mess hall. In between shifts at work, I limped from one military doctor to the next. An initial misdiagnosis by my primary care physician sent me on a wild goose chase of treatments that took several months to run its course. I remember distinctly a trip I made to the podiatry clinic at Walter Reed, to fill a prescription for orthotics. Two weeks earlier molds of my feet were taken, and now I was returning to the hospital to pick up the finished products. When the nurse brought them out for me, I thought he was playing a practical joke.

"There must be some mistake." I looked askance at the two plaster bricks he held out in front of me.

"You're Corporal Mauer, right?"

I nodded.

"Then there's no mistake." He handed me the orthotics, which I almost dropped because they were so unwieldy.

As I sat down in the waiting room to try them on, I was convinced the whole thing was a hoax; I kept looking over at the check-in counter to see if the nurse or any of the other staff was furtively watching and snickering. After several unsuccessful attempts to insert the orthotics into my shoes, I gave up. Not even my combat boots, it occurred to me, would accommodate such devices.

I realized then that my military doctors were incapable of helping me, so I turned to private podiatrists, orthopedists, and neurologists and even paid the expenses out of my own rather shallow pockets. None of it did any good, however. Eventually all of my doctors, private as well military, threw up their collective hands. There was nothing they could do for me, they said. I would just have to live with it—whatever *it* was. In the end, I was told perfunctorily that I had a severe case of flat feet and that I never should have been allowed into the military, as if I might find comfort in knowing that my health problems could have been averted in some alternate reality.

It was shortly after the injury's onset that my primary care physician put me on light duty and offered to submit paperwork for a medical discharge. I chose not to accept the offer because I didn't want to jeopardize my recent acceptance into the University of Virginia. I also wasn't keen on experiencing the stigma associated with a medical discharge, which in the eyes of the Marine Corps was only a short step above a dishonorable one.

When Staff Sergeant Stoke got word of my light duty, he immediately became suspicious of me. As part of the light duty, I was allowed to wear running shoes instead of the normal combat boots with my camouflage uniform, and Stoke took personal offense at this, as if I were trying to sabotage the orderliness of our unit. He branded me a slacker. At first, he showed his displeasure by being curt. Then things escalated.

One morning while I was convalescing in my barracks room after a night shift, the phone rang. The two-block walk from the office earlier had caused me a great deal of pain, and so now I practically crawled out of bed to answer the phone.

It was Stoke. "We need to talk," he said. The tone in his

voice was menacing.

I have always been reticent, and that reticence intensifies when I am faced with confrontation. At such moments I often temporarily suffer from dim-wittedness and entirely lose my capacity to think. So when Stoke said we needed to talk, with an edge to his voice, I turned mute and let *him* do the talking. I suspected the topic of discussion would be my health problems, but never did I imagine the extent to which my situation fueled his contempt. He proceeded to tell me that he found my light-duty status to be a farce. He wouldn't stand for it, he said. I was a disgrace to my unit, to the Marine Corps, and, worst of all, to my country. He wouldn't allow any further embarrassment. For starters, I would have to stop wearing running shoes with my camis ASAP. What must the Commandant of the Marine Corps and the other Joint Chiefs of Staff think upon seeing me "out of uniform"? It simply wouldn't *do*.

My instinct to defend myself, to strike back, gave me a sudden eloquence. "Shouldn't you give me the benefit of the doubt?" I blurted out. "Suppose for a moment my injury is real, that everything I've said is true. What then? *I'll* tell you what: your suggestion that I've fabricated the whole thing would be ludicrous. Anyway, that's beside the point because you don't have the authority to contravene my doctors."

The other end went silent. Stoke clearly hadn't expected this any more than I had, especially not the big words. He muttered something about my not having heard the end of it and abruptly hung up the phone.

Sometime afterward, he made good on his threat. I was scheduled to be discharged in September of that year, but because the fall semester at the University of Virginia began in August, I either would have to apply for an early release or use the vacation days I had saved up so I could be in Charlottesville on time. I decided on the latter option. It still would require approval from my commanding officer, but it would be less of an administrative hassle. Stoke, however, used his influence with the CO to get my vacation denied.

I wasn't sure what to do. It was bad enough that I could hardly walk; now I was confronted with the possibility of not being able to attend UVA because of a technicality. I concluded I had no choice but to go over my CO's head.

Fortunately, the first sergeant at Headquarters Marine Corps had the final say on vacation and discharge requests and, after a short interview with me, took my side in the matter. I remember First Sergeant Emerson fondly. He was one of those thoughtful and fair-minded people who have the ability to restore one's shattered faith in humanity. After he overturned my CO's decision, I figured that that would be the end of the story. But when Stoke heard the news, he became furious. He personally followed up the original vacation denial with a written claim that our unit would experience undue hardship if I were to leave a month early. First Sergeant Emerson apparently wanted all the facts to be straight in his mind before making a decision. He asked Stoke and me to meet with him in his office.

Stoke and I arrived for the meeting at the same time. I gave him a half-hearted smile. He, on the other hand, took the more passive-aggressive route and snubbed me by pretending I wasn't there. We stood at the office door waiting to be called in, avoiding each other's eyes.

First Sergeant Emerson was perusing a document at his desk. He apologized and asked us to wait while he finished. When he finally did, he looked up and smiled broadly. "Have a seat, gentlemen." He gestured for us to sit in the chairs in front of his desk. "I take it you both understand why you're here?"

I nodded, while Stoke replied with an honorific "Yes, sir." His whole demeanor changed in the presence of the first sergeant.

"Let's start with you, Staff Sergeant." First Sergeant Emerson shuffled some papers on his desk. "You've suggested that the use of vacation time by Corporal Mauer would be untenable for you and your staff. Explain to me again your reasons for that."

Stoke hemmed and hawed about the extra hours his staff would have to put in during the four weeks before my replacement arrived from Guam. All the while First Sergeant Emerson smiled wryly. Finally he cut Stoke short, turned to me, and asked what I thought of it all.

I said that if I couldn't start at UVA in the fall, it would mean I would have to reapply for the following year and risk not getting in.

"Well, Staff Sergeant, what do you say to that?" The first sergeant didn't wait for Stoke to reply. "It seems to me to be fair, you have to weigh the benefit of having Corporal Mauer stay on the extra month to you and your staff—which equates to fewer hours—with the cost of having him stay on that month—which might mean not being accepted into the university of his choice. What do you think, Staff Sergeant? Should we play with Corporal Mauer's future just to save you and your staff a few hours' work?"

Stoke remained silent, his gaze fixed on the paperwork on the first sergeant's desk.

"I'll take that as a *no*." The first sergeant stood up, and Stoke and I followed suit. "You'll have my decision in writing by the close of business. Good day, Staff Sergeant." He shook Stoke's hand. To me he said, "Stay back a moment, Corporal, if you wouldn't mind."

After Stoke had gone, the first sergeant closed the door. We sat down again and he said, "This sort of thing happens all the time, unfortunately. Senior staff abusing their authority. Sorry you had to experience it firsthand." It was his duty, he said, to prevent such abuses of power whenever he could. He was especially glad to be helpful in my case. "You have a bright future ahead of you, Corporal." He wished me luck at UVA.

I thanked him profusely before I left.

In the days that followed, I wondered at Stoke's antipathy toward me, which seemed particularly hostile even by Marine Corps standards. Later, I discovered that he had the mistaken impression I concocted the whole story of my ankle problem simply to evade an upcoming physical fitness test. The irony was that I was one of the most fit Marines, if not *the* most fit Marine, in our unit. Stoke must have known the extent to which I enjoyed running, so for him to accuse me of trying to get out of a physical fitness test, when I gladly would have taken it if I could have, was doubly insulting.

My righteous indignation at being falsely accused notwithstanding, I spent the last few months with my Marine Corps unit under a cloud of suspicion. A bad impression, once formed, is hard to live down. Still, I thought it wouldn't hurt to try to clear the air before I left for Charlottesville. So early one morning in the middle of August, even though it caused me pain to do so, I sought out Stoke to say goodbye and to make a last-ditch appeal to his goodwill.

He was in the mess hall eating alone at one of the back tables. I hesitated a moment before approaching him. I still wasn't sure what I was going to say. He hadn't exactly endeared himself to me, after all. Also, at the moment, he didn't appear to be in a mood to talk. He sat there poking at his food with a fork, his head hanging down over the breakfast tray like a prisoner unreconciled to his fate. Thin bands of sunlight seeped through the slats of the blinds behind him and backlit his shaved head.

I slowly made my way to his table. I stood in front of him for a few seconds before he looked up at me with a blank stare, as if he didn't recognize me.

"Oh," he said finally, "it's you."

"I'm going to UVA tomorrow, and I thought—"

"Have a safe trip," he said before I could finish. He reached across the table and gave me a limp-fish handshake, then went back to poking at his food.

I walked away feeling deflated. That wasn't the sort of peace offering I had had in mind.

The next day my discharge from the Marine Corps came and went without fanfare, and I left for Charlottesville with a sense of excitement tempered by despair. I had been looking forward to college for a long time. Before arriving at UVA, I imagined myself on the school's well-manicured Grounds, simultaneously studying and communing with nature, perhaps reading *The Sorrows of Young Werther* on a bench in the shade of a sweetgum tree in one of the Lawn's pavilion gardens, experiencing that heady rush that so often accompanies the consumption of a good book in pleasing surroundings. But my health problems overshadowed this.

For several months after my arrival in Charlottesville, I was in and out of medical clinics. I tried everything: physical therapy, a tens unit, more orthotics, X-rays, steroid injections, a bone scan, a CT scan, an MRI, electric shock treatment, drug cocktails. Since none of these things proved helpful, I was forced to find other ways of minimizing pain. Mainly I just stayed off my feet. I took baths instead of showers. I urinated sitting down. I knelt on a chair or sat on a stool to shave, brush my teeth, and do things in the kitchen. I avoided long lines, to the point that I did most of my shopping late at night when few people were around. At Kroger, I collected my groceries using one of those electric shopping carts reserved for the elderly and the disabled, not caring that people eyed me as if I were playing a fraternity prank. I used a wheelchair on Grounds whenever I could. And whenever I couldn't, I resorted to orthopedic shoes and a cane, hobbling to my classes like a decrepit old man.

I ended up at UVA's pain clinic midway through my first semester. I felt like a guinea pig there. The attending physician, Dr. Graves, put me through a gauntlet of different therapies. At one point, after everything else failed, he suggested I try a lumbar sympathetic nerve block. He had already ruled out sciatica, but there was a possibility I had some other nervous-system disorder. I thought perhaps he was on to something. I took the earliest appointment for the procedure, which was in two weeks' time, in early April. Every day that I had to wait for it seemed like an eternity. I remember thinking that the first thing I would do once I returned to health would be to go for a long hike in the Blue Ridge Mountains near Charlottesville, stretching my disused leg muscles and taking in the scenery.

At last the day for the procedure came. I arrived early for my appointment and filled out some paperwork. After a short wait, I was ushered into a large examination room, with a couple of sophisticated-looking computer monitors on a stand at the end of a hospital bed. Dr. Graves and one of his interns were there, fidgeting with the monitors' controls. They greeted me and went about their business. Then a nurse came in and attached an IV to my wrist, after which I was asked to lie prostrate on the bed with my hospital gown open at the back. One of the machines was a real-time X-ray unit and, according to Dr. Graves, would be used to get the correct positioning for the anesthesia. Once the initial X-ray scan was complete, the intern gently swabbed the identified area of my spine with antimicrobial soap and alcohol. The needle soon followed; I barely felt it enter my back. I watched the needle expertly navigate my spine on the X-ray monitor.

As Dr. Graves injected the drug, he asked me how I was doing.

"Fine," I said. "Should I be feeling anything yet? Or *not* feeling anything, I guess?" I had been told beforehand that it would be a good sign if the pain in my ankles were to diminish upon receiving the anesthetic. But so far nothing had changed.

"Give it some time," Dr. Graves said, and I thought I saw him glance at the intern.

After the procedure, I was escorted by the nurse to the clinic's waiting room and given an apple juice and some graham crackers. I ate and drank mechanically.

Half an hour later still nothing had changed. A sinking feeling came over me. Without waiting for the nurse to dismiss me, I left the clinic and headed for University Avenue, where the restaurants were stirring back to life in anticipation of the lunch hour. Outside, it was gray and overcast, and overhead clouds threatened the first rains of spring. I crossed Jefferson Park Avenue and took a shortcut past the medical school and along the back side of the South Lawn in the direction of the Rotunda. The Grounds were awash with color, dogwood and redbud blossoms in full bloom. By the time I reached University Avenue, my ankles were killing me, despite my geriatric pace and the use of a cane. I stopped for a moment and sat on a bench at a bus stop to recover. Other students passed by, riding bikes or on foot, in front of the shops and restaurants along the street. They all had carefree looks on their faces, and this made me think of how long it had been since I myself experienced the simple pleasure of a jaunt in a commercial district on a lazy spring day. I felt a prick of envy. I would have welcomed any kind of respite from the pain, however short. Then a darker thought occurred to me: there was something mildly absurd about it all, these happy-go-lucky people going about their daily lives, completely oblivious to the pain and emotional upheaval of others around them. I had the urge to shout at them, to tell them to wake up. For many of them, it was only a matter of time before they, too, would experience chronic pain; age would do to them what genetics did to me.

In a daze, I got up from the bench, crossed the street, and went into The Virginian and straight to the bar. I needed a drink, something hard like a shot of peppermint schnapps. I lied as I placed the order and said I had just done brilliantly an exam and wanted to celebrate. The bartender congratulated me and gave me a second shot on the house. I downed both drinks along with three more in quick succession before leaving the restaurant.

I lurched into the midday air. The weather had improved, the sun just beginning to emerge from behind a black cloud. As I approached the street, I felt a sense of exhilaration, as if a great weight had been lifted from my shoulders. The alcohol had numbed my ankle pain; I was invincible. Hurriedly I looked left, then right. I discerned the outlines of cars moving toward me on both sides of the street. *I dare you*, I thought, hearing a horn honking in the distance. Or was it closer by? Damned if I cared. I stepped onto the street carelessly. The honking continued, but I ignored it. A guy at the bus stop yelled something unintelligible, reached out to put a hand on my arm. I shrugged him off before he was able. "Mind your own," I said and trailed off uncertainly. Own your mind? Did I really say that? The mind playing tricks. Like a false echo. At its periphery, the Rotunda showed double for a second, then became whole again as I went by. Unsteadily I made my way down one of the colonnades of the Lawn until I reached the Homer statue in front of Cabell Hall. In the shade of a large ash tree, using my backpack as a pillow, I passed out for an hour or more, as blind as Homer to the too-vivid world around me.

I swore off doctors for a while after that. To preoccupy my mind in the meantime, I devoutly studied and attended classes, which were going well in spite of my circumstances. A full class load would have been physically impossible for me, so each semester I took only four classes. It was expensive to do this, as the G.I. Bill lasted only so many months, but I had no choice. As luck would have it, right before I was discharged from the Marine Corps, I had an exit interview with a Veterans Affairs representative who advised me to apply for a special program for disabled veterans under which all college expenses would be paid in full. I applied for the program without any expectation of success. Near the end of my first semester at UVA, however, a letter arrived from the regional VA office in Roanoke. At first I couldn't think of what it could be, unless it was a summons to the Richmond VA hospital for a checkup. I often received such letters because of my disability status, so it wouldn't have been out of the ordinary for this latest letter to relate to that. Then I remembered my application to the VA program, and I felt a twinge of excitement. I tore open the envelope, giving myself a paper cut in the process. As I unfolded the letter, a large smear of blood appeared on its outer edge, like some perverse ornamental seal. I disregarded the cut and read the letter, which informed me to my delight that I had been accepted into the VA program conditional on a meeting with a counselor in the Roanoke office during the upcoming winter break.

Days passed, school let out, and winter tightened its grip. The night before the VA meeting, a severe storm hit. I awoke to find everything outside covered in snow and ice. It was bitterly cold. My ankles were worse than usual. To minimize pain throughout the drive to Roanoke, I removed my shoes and pinned my legs up against the underside of the steering column. I couldn't avoid using my right foot to accelerate and brake during intra-city driving, but on I-81, I was able to set the cruise control and never once apply pressure to my ankles. The tableau I presented was absurd, and yet it didn't matter. The prospect of getting a full ride to school had put me in an expansive mood. I wasn't going to let my health problems defeat me. I would do something important with my life, perhaps become a writer. And the VA program would be a turning point to that end.

On I-81, I lowered the driver's side window a crack. Freezing cold air gushed in. I didn't care. Wagner's opera *Das Rheingold* was playing on the stereo, the Vienna Philharmonic Orchestra version. I turned up the volume. Scene 2 had just started. In it, Wotan, the king of the gods, is asleep with his wife on a mountaintop. Dreaming, he bellows out in his bass-baritone voice: "The sacred dwelling of joy / is guarded by gate and door: / Manhood's honor, might without bound, / rise now to endless renown." It was all the encouragement I needed. My dreams could come true, I thought, if only I set my mind to them—mind over body, so to speak. I dropped my legs from under the steering column to stretch. The pain in my ankles had lessened. I closed the window. A mileage sign along the highway read 80 miles to Roanoke.

I reached the VA office by mid-morning. The snow and ice on the roads had turned to slush. I switched off the stereo and pulled into the deserted parking lot. My whole body ached as I got out of the car. The cold air made it worse. I went to the trunk, removed my wheelchair, and rolled through the automatic doors of the building. Except for a single security guard, who simply nodded as I entered, the lobby was deserted, as well.

I took the elevator up to the seventh floor. The doors opened and I wheeled out. To one side of the elevator bank stood a copy machine and a series of large gray metal filing cabinets. On a cork bulletin board above the copier hung an inspirational calendar, which contained blurbs on the lives of paraplegics and amputees who succeeded against the odds. It was now December, but the month of October was still being displayed. At the top of the October page, a quotation read: "Your ability to succeed is a direct reflection of your ability to try." Apparently the words weren't enough to inspire the VA staff to turn the pages of the calendar.

The seventh floor had an open floor plan that was dotted with cubicles and desks. At one of the desks, the VA counselor sat waiting for me. He glanced at my wheelchair as I approached. "You must be Andrew Mauer," he said. He didn't get up.

I stopped a few feet short of his desk. "I'm Andrew, yes." I scanned the office space to see if any other people were around. It seemed we had the entire floor to ourselves.

"My name is Harold Kane." The counselor glanced at my wheelchair again. "I've been assigned to finalize your case. I hope you didn't have too much trouble getting here. The roads were a bit treacherous this morning."

I told him my drive from Charlottesville had been fine.

On his desk in front of him lay a manila folder, which I presumed was my case file. He opened it and read to himself while I watched. Something in my file seemed to be bothering him. For over a minute he scrutinized the same page. I was getting tired of looking at the odd figure he cut. I couldn't make out his trousers or his shoes from behind the desk, but his polyester oxford shirt was one of those multi-colored pinstripe affairs that had been out of fashion for years. He wore a regimental-stripe necktie that clashed with his shirt. He also had sideburns, and his graying hair was long and unkempt. He looked like a throwback to the Seventies.

He closed the folder. "So it's your ankles, is it, that necessitates the use of *that*?" He gestured vaguely toward my wheelchair.

"Yes," I said, "if I understand what you're asking." I mentioned the trouble I had been having walking but with little elaboration. I didn't want him to think I was exaggerating my health problems or my need for the VA's assistance.

"I see," he said. Then he stood up suddenly and asked me to follow him to a window. There, he looked down into the parking lot and began to tell a story of a veteran, not unlike myself, who had applied a few years earlier for the same VA program I had. "I'm struck by the similarities between the two of you," Mr. Kane said. "This other veteran must have been about your age. He hailed from somewhere in the Midwest, just like you. And on the day of our meeting about his application, he, too, showed up in a wheelchair."

Mr. Kane paused, as if to allow his words to sink in.

"It has been awhile since all this happened," he went on, "but I think the veteran's last name was Clark. Or maybe it was Clay. Anyhow, Clay or Clark, whichever it was, claimed to have something wrong with his spine, which severely limited his ability to walk. His medical records were in order and corroborated his claim, and so it never occurred to me to doubt anything he said about his disability. By the time our meeting ended that day, I had every intention of signing off on his application—until I saw something that changed my mind. Down there." He pointed at the parking lot below us. "I was standing at this very window, like you and I are now, taking a break after my meeting and drinking a cup of coffee, when I saw Clark—or whatever the punk's name was—get up out of his wheelchair and walk the fifty feet to his car without skipping a beat." Mr. Kane looked at me triumphantly.

I didn't know what to say. What *could* I say? I couldn't be rude to him, the man who held my future in his hands, and, to be honest, at the time I had only a vague sense that he was accusing me of something. I just sat there in my wheelchair, blankly staring at him.

When I didn't respond, he launched into a lecture on the arbitrariness and injustice of the VA decision-making process. He appeared to have a gripe about a nephew of his whose application for VA benefits had been denied. I couldn't see what this had to do with me. Then Mr. Kane said, "By all rights, you never should have been approved for the VA program. My nephew should have. But my boss, who has the final say, was adamant you get approval. If it had been up to me …"

He didn't finish his sentence, but he didn't need to. I understood perfectly what he was saying. My only question was, why was he saying it? Did he expect me to feel sorry for him? I didn't give a damn about his nephew. I wanted to tell him as much, but I couldn't. As I sat there looking down into the parking lot, it dawned on me that what I was going through was all a game, and that to get what I wanted, I had to play along, perhaps pretend I was equally outraged by the injustice against Mr. Kane's nephew, or at a minimum disguise my own happiness about the VA's decision in my case. In the end, I did what I usually do under such circumstances. I said nothing.

Mr. Kane had a defeated expression on his face as he escorted me back to the lobby. Before we parted, I thanked him, and only partly facetiously. In spite of his treatment of me, I couldn't find it in myself to hold a grudge against him. He had been the messenger of good tidings, after all.

But back in Charlottesville, I began to seethe at what Mr. Kane said to me. Not only had he questioned my integrity, but apparently he also had tried to get my VA application denied so that he could engage in nepotism. The nerve of the guy, and after everything I had gone through. I wanted to punch him or, better yet, spit in his face. It would serve him right. For days after the meeting in Roanoke, I obsessed over the idea of exacting revenge, replaying in my mind alternate versions of my encounter with Mr. Kane, each one involving varying degrees of violence against him. Uppermost in my mind was a desire to prove him wrong about my need for a wheelchair. I contemplated writing him a letter, with additional supporting documents from my doctors. But I knew that would be futile. Mr. Kane didn't care about the truth any more than I cared about his nephew. And the VA as an organization was like a black hole into which things, like the contents of an unsolicited letter, could be drawn and never see the light of day again.

The more I brooded over my experiences with Mr. Kane, the more they became connected in my mind with what I had suffered at the hands of Staff Sergeant Stoke, as if the two men were in cahoots. On their own, the separate experiences could be viewed as isolated incidents. But taken together they suggested a pattern. People, I began to realize, didn't always act in good faith. By turns they could be self-serving, petty, or vindictive. And if others could be that way, so could I. What was to prevent me from giving Kane or Stoke a taste of his own medicine? How exactly I might go about that, I wasn't sure. But whatever I did, it would have to be dramatic, perhaps a prank involving some sort of fecal twist. Then something occurred to me. In the contacts of my smartphone, I still had Stoke's home phone number and address. I didn't have the energy or the will to post a letter—containing, say, a dollop of shit—but I could call Stoke and gloat about my full ride and other successes at UVA. It would be brilliant, not to mention spectacularly juvenile.

I executed my plan a few weeks later. One evening, upon

returning to my apartment after watching a BBC film production of *Macbeth* assigned for a class, I called Stoke. The film had been shown in the basement of Clemons Library. The violence of the play along with the gloomy and claustrophobic atmosphere of the viewing room had put me in a sanguine mood. I could smell blood in the air as I dialed Stoke's number.

His wife answered. She must have been aware of my falling out with Stoke because she hesitated when I told her who I was. "Hang on a second," she said. A crinkling sound came over the line, as if she had put a hand to the phone's mouthpiece. In the background, I could hear muffled voices. Nearly a minute passed. I was getting worried. I hadn't come all this way for my plan to backfire simply because Stoke refused to talk to me.

Finally he picked up the phone. "This is Staff Sergeant Stoke." His voice quavered.

"Hello, Staff Sergeant," I said, a little too enthusiastically. "It's Andrew Mauer."

"I know," he said, and from his tone it was clear that what he really meant was, "Yes, I know, so why are you calling me?"

As nonchalantly as I could, I asked him how things were going at Headquarters Marine Corps.

"Good," was all he said.

I expected him to ask how *I* was doing, but he didn't. So I volunteered the information. I said I had earned a 4.0 in my classes during the fall semester, and because of it, I had been awarded a full-ride scholarship. I followed this up with as many half-truths as I could think of.

"I really should be—" he started to say at one point, but I kept talking.

Before he hung up on me, I recounted the details of my health problems—the numerous medical appointments, the orthopedic shoes, the cane, the wheelchair, the late-night escapades at Kroger—but I also embellished here and there, indicating, for example, that my doctors had concluded surgery would be the only way for me to ever walk normally again. I hadn't intended the lies; they just came to me of their own accord, like flesh to the scalpel. My original intention had been to make Stoke jealous of my situation at school. Now, I wanted nothing more than to make him feel guilty for the way he had treated me. And to do so, I couldn't very well tell him the truth: that my doctors were baffled by my condition and still couldn't give me a definitive diagnosis. It might cast doubt in Stoke's mind. Lying merely simplified things.

Little did I know at the time how much truth there would end up being in my lies, how five years later I would undergo the very surgery I invented on the spur of the moment to serve my purposes on the call with Stoke. That was just my luck. Even my lies, told out of spite, weren't really lies at all. So much for my foray into the dark world of subterfuge.

Nine years passed before my ankles healed on their own. Slowly, year by year—at times the changes as imperceptible as the movement of a glacier—I regained the ability to walk without pain. Like Charlie Gordon in *Flowers for Algernon*, I was granted a new lease on life, even if I wasn't the same person I had been before. How could I possibly be the same person after being a semi-invalid for a decade? During that time, my muscles atrophied to such an extent, I stood with a slight hunch, my legs as shriveled as an octogenarian's. And of course, I developed other health problems as well. Just as Charlie Gordon's transformation into an intellectual genius was too good to be true, so was my new lease on life.

I would be remiss if I didn't mention that during the intervening years between my college graduation and my ankle recovery, I went through several more unnecessary medical procedures, including surgery. Unlike at UVA, however, for the more recent procedures, I wasn't alone. My wife Sarasi was there. After my surgery—which was ill-conceived and which left me with an odd, uneven-legged gait—she was there for me. She was there for me, too, when I developed other health problems. And later, when I broke down mentally, under circumstances that would have tried the patience of a saint and at a time when I had absolutely no right to expect it of her, Sarasi was there for me.

She and I first met in graduate school at Georgetown University in D.C. The MBA program we were in offered a two-week prep course, and as fate would have it, we both enrolled. I was attracted to Sarasi from the first moment I saw her. I didn't know then that she was of Sri Lankan descent, but I suspected early on that she was South Asian.

A few weeks into graduate school I asked her out on a date, and she accepted. I planned an elaborate evening to impress her: a Beethoven concert at the Kennedy Center followed by dinner at the Roof Terrace Restaurant. The VA was still paying my way through school, so I had money to burn.

The night of our date I met Sarasi in the foyer of her apartment building in Foggy Bottom. She was sitting on a bench near the entryway waiting for me when the doorman let me in. She had on a sleeveless salmon-colored tunic with gray leggings and a pashmina shawl. Her hair was pulled back into a fishtail braid. She wasn't wearing any makeup, but then, she didn't need to. Even without it, she looked chic and sophisticated.

"You look wonderful," I said.

"Thank you." She stood up, smiling shyly. As if apologizing, she added, "I wasn't sure how much I should dress up."

"I wouldn't change a thing," I said and offered her my arm.

At the Kennedy Center, we took our seats in the concert hall's orchestra section. I could feel the excitement in the air as the conductor signaled to the orchestra members to tune their instruments on the lead oboist's A. I had been looking forward to the performance myself for quite a while. I considered Beethoven to be a kindred spirit. We both suffered from a physical disability, and we both, in our own ways, had tortured souls. I wanted to articulate as much to Sarasi but chose not to for fear of scaring her.

The concert began with Beethoven's Fifth. Like the hammer blows of fate, the horns announced the piece in an intense four-note rhythm. Then with a softening and a quickening of pace, the stringed instruments took over. Just as quickly, the horns burst forth again in a variation on the opening bars. There was something ominous about Beethoven's transitions.

I took Sarasi's hand in mine. She smiled without taking her eyes off the stage. She seemed enraptured by the music. And in the dim light of the concert hall, she was even more beautiful than when I picked her up at her apartment. She looked in profile like the foremost girl in Amrita Sher-Gil's painting *Three Girls*, with her large almond eyes and full lips and perfectly sculpted eyebrows. I was tempted to kiss her.

Instead, I let go of her hand and surreptitiously reached down and undid the laces of my shoes. My feet had gone numb. I held my breath as the oboe cadenza intruded into the first movement of the symphony like a mournful cry for help.

The music played on, oscillating between darkness and light. From the explosive fragments of its opening, the Fifth transitioned into the slow, lyrical second movement, which in turn transitioned into the shadowy world of the scherzo and, from there, into the blaring horns of the finale. The kettledrums beat as the violins' arpeggios climbed to a crescendo. Gradually the full orchestra joined in, and the piece ended in a forceful fortissimo. As the last notes drifted into nothingness, the audience erupted in a frenzy of applause.

All around me people crowded in. Whispers passed from their lips like accusations. The stage lights flickered and dimmed. Before I knew it, the orchestra was playing the middle movement of Beethoven's "Ghost" piano trio. At the point when the cello and piano decouple and the violin makes its entrance, I nearly wept. I lifted my legs and pinned them against the seat in front of me. The piano figurations were becoming increasingly eerie. I closed my eyes. For a fleeting moment in my mind a spectral vision came and went. When I opened my eyes again, the song had ended. The ghostly mist of Beethoven's feigned rescue lingered in the air.

I placed my feet back onto the floor. Sarasi appeared not to have noticed my agitation; her eyes remained fixed on the stage throughout the trio's last movement.

The chandeliers and wall sconces came on. Sarasi excused herself to go to the restroom while I stayed back. I could hardly move. Trancelike I watched people vacate their seats one by one, the haunting pulse of "Ghost" reverberating in my mind.

I sensed rather than saw the seats of the concert hall slowly re-fill, only half-registered Sarasi's smile and her delicate brush against my knee as she went by.

Then it came, after the lights dimmed, the long-awaited Ninth. It was beauty incarnate, from first to last. The opening was pure atmosphere and suspense. It drew me out of myself. During the scherzo, I looked up at the honeycombed ceiling and very clearly saw myself running along the Potomac, just running and running, all light and air. No one, nothing, could catch me. I was whole again. And then there was the slow movement and the singing last movement, first the winds and brass clearing the air and then the cellos and basses speaking to each other like long-lost brothers and finally the chorus and solo vocalists going on and on about joy joy joy.

For the ovation I stood like everyone else. Amid the commotion, I leaned over and kissed Sarasi on the cheek. Evidently she was in as good a mood as I was; as we left the concert hall and made our way upstairs to the restaurant, I heard her humming the "Ode to Joy."

"You liked the concert, then?" I asked.

She said she did. Very much.

At the restaurant, the maitre d' led us to our table. For a minute or two before the waiter arrived, neither of us spoke. We sat there fidgeting with our napkins and silverware and sipping from our water glasses until eventually Sarasi broke the silence.

"Tell me what it was like growing up in Kansas," she said. "I don't know the first thing about that part of the country."

"You haven't missed much."

"You can't mean that."

"Sure I do." I set down my water glass. "I grew up in a place called Cawker City. Population: 400. Everyone there knows everyone else. I couldn't wait to leave. And do you know what its claim to fame is?"

"Should I?"

"I hope not," I said. "It would be odd if you did."

The waiter interrupted us and took our orders.

After he had gone, Sarasi asked, "Well, what is it? Cawker City's claim to fame?"

"It boasts the world's largest ball of twine."

She laughed. "You're teasing me."

"If only I were," I said. In my haste to leave the concert hall, I forgot to re-tie my shoes. I slipped them off now. I was starting to sweat. "What about you?" I asked. "Tell me about *your* childhood."

While we waited for our food, Sarasi regaled me with stories about Sri Lanka. Among other things, she described her life in Colombo, how she was taught by nuns at St. Bridget's Convent and how she later transferred to Visakha Vidyalaya, a Buddhist school for girls, to take her O and A levels. Then two months shy of her eighteenth birthday, she came to the States to attend Smith College.

I knew very little about Sri Lanka other than that it used to be called Ceylon and that, like India and other parts of South Asia, it had been colonized by the British. Sarasi's stories helped fill in some of the gaps in my knowledge. "A convent," I said. "Does that mean you're Catholic?"

"No. I'm Buddhist, although I don't consider myself a practicing one."

The waiter brought our food. Sarasi and I put our napkins onto our laps. I used the opportunity, when she wasn't looking, to dab the sweat from my face.

"Is there anything else I can get you?" the waiter asked, stepping back from our table.

"A bottle of wine would be good," I said. I looked at Sarasi. "What do you say?"

"I'd love some."

I handed the waiter the wine list. "The South African merlot, please." Then I turned back to Sarasi. "We were talking about St. Bridget's. So the British tried to convert Sri Lanka to Christianity?"

"Yes. And the Portuguese and the Dutch before them." Each of the three European powers, she said, occupied Sri Lanka at roughly 150-year intervals, like a tag-team relay, and left behind their religions, their languages, their food, their music, their sports, even their genes. St. Bridget's was just one of many remnants of the country's colonization that spanned nearly five centuries.

I found it fascinating to hear about Sri Lanka's fusion of European and South Asian cultures. One of Sarasi's stories about St. Bridget's in particular struck my fancy. As she told it, I pictured her and the other Bridgetines in their freshly starched uniforms on the grounds of the convent, which was housed in old Spanish-style buildings with terracotta-tile roofs and sprawling white verandas. Apparently every school-day morning, the mother superior would assemble the children for the Lord's Prayer in the auditorium. They were a motley group, Sarasi said: an elderly Tamil woman in her white nun's habit and black veil with the demeanor of a drill instructor, rows upon rows of brown-skinned girls of various ethnicities, ages, and religions standing at attention in their stiff white dresses. Few of the girls wanted to participate in the prayer, least of all the Christian ones. Each morning in the auditorium they would stand there unsure of themselves, the Christian children half-smirking and looking at one another peripherally, the Muslim children and Sarasi and the other Buddhist children squirming and making faces as if they had mouthfuls of bitter melon.

"I complain now," Sarasi said upon finishing her story, "but I don't regret my time at St. Bridget's. It made it easier for me to acclimate when I got to Smith."

I admitted that I didn't know how I would have fared myself if the tables had been turned, if I had had to go to college abroad. "It wouldn't have been easy for me, I know that much. I've never even been outside of the United States before. In the Marine Corps, I had the chance to be stationed in Scotland or Guam, but I chose Virginia instead." I was going to add that it would have been especially difficult for me to attend college abroad seeing how I was a cripple, but I bit my tongue.

"We'll have to fix that," Sarasi said. Before she could explain what she meant, the waiter arrived with our bottle of wine.

He uncorked it, poured each of us a quarter glass, and waited a moment while I swirled and tasted mine. It smelled of mulberries and black cherries and potpourri.

"It's excellent," I said.

The waiter smiled and left.

I raised my glass. "To a joyous evening."

"To a joyous evening," Sarasi echoed.

Our glasses clinked in the flickering candlelight.

Subsequent to that night, Sarasi and I went on several more dates. They were less elaborate than the first one, but each time I succeeded in impressing her, and each time I went to extraordinary lengths to keep my health problems a secret. It wasn't long, however, before she discovered the truth. As much as I wanted to, I couldn't hide it from her. I had no choice, really; despite my deceitfulness with Staff Sergeant Stoke, I wasn't by nature a liar.

It was sometime in April. The cherry blossoms were in bloom. I was feeling particularly despondent because I would be missing the festivities on the Mall. That morning, while preparing for school, I experienced a flare up so severe, I was compelled to skip classes. Sarasi called to find out what happened, and it was then I told her everything. Not surprisingly, she wanted to know why I had been so secretive.

"It's complicated," I said.

"Try me."

"Okay. For one thing, I'm sick of talking about my health problems. The self-pity reaches a saturation point and then becomes nauseating. As for the pain itself, and don't take this the wrong way, you can't possibly understand it"—as I said this, images of myself riding a cart at Kroger and hobbling about the UVA Grounds with a cane flashed through my mind like a movie montage—"not because of any failing on your part but because of the difficulty of truly understanding someone else's pain. Even my doctors don't get it, and they're paid to."

"Maybe I don't understand," she said, "but that doesn't mean I can't sympathize. It also doesn't justify your secrecy."

"No, but my fear about how you might react *does*."

"And how might I react?"

"I don't know, that's the problem." The words came out harshly, disproportionate to the circumstances. My fear of her reaction was the real crux of the matter. But instead of confronting that fear head on, I found myself wanting to back away from it, to irrationally blame someone else for it.

A minute went by in silence.

Eventually I said, rather cryptically, "I've been burned before."

"Meaning?"

"Meaning, I was afraid you might jump ship if you found out the truth."

She sighed. "You don't know me very well."

I didn't respond immediately. Her words had struck a nerve because they were true in more ways than one. It occurred to me that I *didn't* know her very well, and if anyone was to blame, it was me, not her. In the time we had spent together, I had been reluctant to fully devote myself to our relationship. "I have my reasons," I said by way of apology. I told her about the short-lived relationships I had had with women at UVA. "I'll never forget the parting words of one of them. 'I'm not strong enough for both of us,' she said. It was pathetic, but at least she had the courtesy to break the news to me in person. Another girlfriend didn't even do that; one day she just started avoiding me. I was left to find out through a third party that she didn't want to see me anymore."

"I'm sorry for that," Sarasi said, "but please don't project the behavior of your past girlfriends onto me." The more we talked, the more conciliatory Sarasi's tone became. She didn't say it in so many words, but the implication was that, come what may, she would take me as I was; that she wasn't like other women; that in essence she was willing to make sacrifices for my sake. Before we got off the phone, she insisted she could be of help to me, her voice trailing off as if she were embarrassed by her overt show of tenderness.

Sadly, I only half-believed her at the time. To me there were few selfless people in the world; Stoke, Kane, and my former girlfriends taught me that. But I soon learned that Sarasi was different. She was no saint, to be sure, but neither was she like anyone I had ever known before. In fact, she was generous and caring in ways that made me feel inadequate. She was, I realized as we continued to date, eminently good for me.

The attraction turned out to be mutual. During our second year of graduate school, we got engaged. I made a point of proposing to her in the most romantic way I could think of. It was October, and the leaves were turning, the maple and oak trees exploding into a kaleidoscope of coppers and oranges and reds and yellows. I called Sarasi and told her to meet me at noon in our favorite spot on the grounds of the National Cathedral. I had a surprise for her, I said.

With a diamond ring in my coat pocket, I set off for the cathedral in high spirits. I took a cab to avoid walking. Serendipitously the driver had Beethoven's Ninth blaring on the stereo the whole way over. He didn't look like a classical-music aficionado to me, what with his Redskins jersey and the gold chain, but who was I to judge?

"That's our song," I said gleefully from the backseat.

The cabdriver just looked at me quizzically in the rearview mirror.

When we got to the cathedral, I paid the driver and went to

the Bishop's Garden and sat on a bench. My watch read 11:57. Any minute Sarasi would arrive.

I waited with a sense of excitement. Everything was going to plan. It was a beautiful day: a cool breeze, sunshine, the garden awash with color. All around were various trees and evergreen shrubs and flowering perennials. A few feet in front of me the velvety purple flowers of a sage cascaded onto the cobblestone walkway; behind me, the weather vane and slate roof of the Shadow House gazebo rose up in their Gothic splendor above a yew tree.

Ten minutes elapsed. Sarasi was late. I got up and walked as far as the cathedral. Tourists were milling about here and there, but there was no sign of Sarasi. Overhead, clouds had appeared. I was heading back to my bench when I heard something tap against the walkway. Little white balls flashed across my field of vision. I looked up, stuck out my hand. A piece of ice hit the fleshy part of my palm and fell to the ground.

The hail came down harder. I could hear people running up behind me.

"You might want to take cover," one of them said as he passed by.

I hurried in their wake to the gazebo. There were three other people taking cover: two priests, one young and one old, and a middle-aged woman. For close to five minutes we listened to the hail battering the gazebo roof.

The hail finally stopped, and it started to sprinkle. Strangely, the sun was shining. I sat on a ledge of the gazebo and buried my head in my hands. From atop the cathedral, the grotesques and gargoyles cackled like devils.

The old priest came over. He wore a black tab-collar shirt. "I don't mean to pry," he said, "but you don't look very happy."

"I was expecting someone," I said and gave him a faint smile.

"Do you mean her?" he asked, pointing out into the garden.

A woman was moving along the walkway. It was Sarasi. Her hair and clothes glistened in the diffuse light.

I thanked the priest and went to her.

She was out of breath, as if she had been running. "I'm so sorry," she said. Her Metro train had been delayed. "Will you ever forgive me?"

"For what?"

She pressed her fingers against the ring box in my pocket and kissed me. "For ruining everything."

"It could have been worse," I said. "You might not have shown up at all."

The two priests and the woman walked by with grins on their faces. "Let's leave these two lovebirds alone," the woman said.

For another minute Sarasi and I stood huddled together in the shimmering rain.

Our wedding took place a year after we started our first jobs in D.C. We had a traditional Sinhalese ceremony in Colombo, with Kandyan dancers and a *poruwa*, a type of dais used in Sinhalese weddings. My in-laws spared no expense, renting out the ballroom of the Hilton. By South Asian standards the wedding was small—only about 350 guests—but to a Westerner from humble origins, the experience was daunting, especially since there was no wedding rehearsal to prepare me for the esoteric Buddhist ceremony. I remember asking my father-in-law Sunil on several occasions when the rehearsal would be, and each time I was told not to worry. "No worries," he would say. "Everything will be fine." I took this to mean that a rehearsal would happen eventually, just not at a prescribed time. But of course, one never did. It was my first of many lessons in Asian evasiveness.

My sister-in-law, Nalika, must have sensed my bewilderment at the wedding. She pulled me aside and slipped me some whiskey a few minutes before Sarasi and I were supposed to enter the ballroom. "Here," she said, a flask appearing as if by magic from beneath the fall of her sari. "You look like you could use this. I stole it from Thathi's suit pocket."

I didn't need any persuading. I sniffed the contents of the flask and then took a pull. The whiskey burned as it went down my throat.

"Don't let it go to your head," she whispered. "That I'm being nice to you, I mean."

"I won't," I said with a laugh. It was good to see her lighten up. Previously, there had been an undercurrent between us. She seemed ambivalent about my appearance on the scene, as if I were deceitfully inveigling my way into her family.

She straightened my bowtie and brushed a piece of lint from the lapel of my coat. "I was thinking," she said, "how under different circumstances you and I might have been more to each other than brother- and sister-in-law."

I couldn't tell whether she was being serious or not. Although she was several years older than Sarasi, she wasn't yet married. She once joked, after I teased her about finding a husband, that there was a shortage of decent Sri Lankan men because of a stagnant gene pool. "The few smart ones left are living in Australia or the UK."

"Why don't you follow them?" I suggested at the time. "Or better yet, find an American."

"Who'd take care of my parents in old age?"

I simply shrugged, the dilemma seemingly an insoluble one.

Now, moments before my own wedding ceremony, I found

myself tongue-tied with Nalika again. The timely arrival of my mother-in-law Lalanthi saved me from having to respond. She poked her head out from behind the ballroom door. "Your presence is required, Andrew."

"I'm coming," I said.

"It's too bad we're not Muslims," Nalika whispered to me. "Then you could marry *both* sisters."

I was tempted to say, half-facetiously, "Yes, if only." Instead, I took another pull of whiskey.

"Good luck." Nalika grabbed the half-empty flask and hid it in her clutch. "You should be going. You don't want to be late for your own wedding."

I leaned over and kissed her, European style. I was feeling nostalgic, perhaps because of the alcohol. Also, I had the rather eupeptic expectation that she would counter with a romantic gesture of some kind, but all I got was a patronizing pat on the arm as she sent me on my way. I felt less like a groom on the verge of marriage than a bleary-eyed child venturing off to his first day of school.

In the ballroom, Sarasi was waiting for me near the *poruwa*. She looked stunning in her delicately embroidered white sari. I gave her an admiring glance and took my position by her side. Hardly had I done so than the Kandyan dancers made their entrance. As I watched them—in their ornate costumes of red, white, and black, with equally ornate headdresses and with long, barrel-shaped wooden drums strapped to their waists— the whiskey began to take its inexorable effect. From that point onward, the proceedings assumed the ethereal character of a fairy tale. The dancers' movements were fluid and stylized, like those of strange gigantic birds in a courtship ritual. I stood there mesmerized. When the performance finally ended, one of Sarasi's great uncles, who had been appointed as an officiant, motioned for us to step onto the *poruwa*.

Even after the effects of the alcohol wore off, I looked on as if through a semi-drunken haze. The events had an air both magical and unreal. Sarasi made eye signals for me to follow her lead as she took from her uncle seven gold coins wrapped in betel leaves and placed them onto the *poruwa*. He tied our pinkies together with a white thread and doused them in water. All the while six little girls (or were there three, and I was seeing double?) chanted Pali verses to bless our union. From one moment to the next, I had no idea what was going on or what I was doing. Only by some bizarre process of perfectly executed improvisation did everything turn out fine, frustratingly just as Sunil had predicted.

The dinner went as smoothly as the ceremony, and afterward Sarasi and I made the rounds through the ballroom, thanking our guests. When we got to Nalika's table, her seat was empty.

"Where's Nalika?" Sarasi asked one of the old aunties at the table.

"I don't know, darling," said the auntie. "No one's seen her since right before the food was served."

"That's strange," Sarasi said.

Beethoven's Ninth started to play, part of the playlist I had given to the DJ. The guests clapped and goaded Sarasi and me to the dance floor. The wondrous Ninth, I thought. I could have kissed everyone in the room.

I took Sarasi by the hand. On our way to the dance floor, I said, "This is our song" to each and every person who cared to listen.

I didn't sleep for two days. Going from D.C. to London to Frankfurt to Dubai took Sarasi and me over thirty hours, and then on the SriLankan Airlines flight to Colombo, my seat had a broken lumbar support so that a piece of metal dug painfully into my lower back. I was a physical and emotional wreck when our plane finally landed at Bandaranaike airport, my body and mind near their respective breaking points. I never should have hazarded the trip, but I thought a month's rest and relaxation away from work would do me good.

Outside the airport terminal, a van was waiting for us. The driver took our bags and stowed them at the back of the vehicle. It was early morning, so traffic was light as we made our way to my in-laws' place in Nawala. That was a consolation, at least; I would be spared a drive down Negombo Road during rush hour. I likely would have vomited if I had had to go through the usual free-for-all of Colombo traffic: trishaws, cars, and trucks alike outrageously ignoring the lane markings, weaving in and out within an inch of one's life, and then abruptly hitting gridlock, starting and stopping every few seconds, starting and stopping, like a roller coaster on the blink.

Along Negombo Road, even fewer people than cars were out and about, only the occasional shopkeeper preparing their wares for the day's sales. Stray dogs, on the other hand, were out in droves. Mangy and slightly rabid-looking, their eyes yellow in the headlights of the oncoming traffic, they littered the streets like so much discarded trash. I turned to Sarasi and said with irritation, "I thought there was a campaign recently to sterilize stray dogs."

"There was." She took in her surroundings with the keen absorption of someone returning home after a long absence. She looked travel-weary but happy, her half-smile giving her an air of contentment that seemed to say, "I'm home again, at last."

"Look," she said suddenly, pointing out the window, and with that, the thread of the conversation I started was lost.

I looked in the direction she had pointed. On a jacaranda tree alongside the road hung more than a dozen white paper lanterns, still alight from the night before. The glow of the lanterns made it possible to see, even in the relative dark, the mass of purple bell-shaped flowers that covered the tree's canopy. It was a happy sight, one that would have lifted my spirits if I hadn't been in such a foul mood.

"And *there*," Sarasi said. Again she pointed out the window, this time at what looked like Christmas lights suspended above the entryway of a Buddhist-temple complex. "Vesak," she said, sounding disappointed. "We just missed it." She meant Vesak Poya Day, the day of the full moon in May. On the Buddhist calendar, every full moon corresponded to a holiday, and Vesak was of particular importance, as it marked the birth, enlightenment, and death of the Buddha. It was analogous to Christmas in the West, except without the crass commercialism. Like Christmas, on Vesak, lights were strung in profusion to celebrate the occasion.

I peered out into the darkness and watched the temple lights recede from view. For the first time, I noticed the moon, full in the western sky. It brought to mind my initial visit to Sri Lanka, shortly before our wedding three years earlier, the one time we had arrived exactly on the day of Vesak. Much had happened since then. In terms of my exposure to Sri Lankan culture, I had become a veteran of sorts. Even so, after four extended stays in the country, I still hadn't grown accustomed to its stark contrasts: the dazzling lights, the bursts of vibrant color, the gracious smiles amid the tropical heat and the generally squalid, dog-infested streets. It was part of my usual response upon arriving in Colombo, the place attracting me at the same time that it repulsed me. When I was here, I couldn't wait to leave; when I wasn't, I couldn't wait to get back.

"Next time we come," I said to Sarasi, simultaneously

thinking of our departure in a month and our return in a year, "shall we schedule an arrival date that coincides with Vesak?"

My question fell on deaf ears. Sarasi was still looking out the window. "It's good to be home."

Upon arriving at my in-laws', I said hello to everyone and then went straight to bed. Something was wrong with my back. No matter what position I tried, I couldn't get comfortable, and I couldn't sleep. For several hours I just lay there in a pool of sweat, even with the ceiling fan on full blast. The guestroom window was open, and I listened alternately to the chirping of squirrels and to the obnoxious calls of the koels and the resident kingfisher.

Later in the day, Sarasi came to check on me.

"I can't move," I said.

She had brought me something to eat and drink, a plate of fish buns and a glass of passion-fruit juice. She set the things onto the side table. "I'm getting worried," she said. "Maybe we should make an appointment for you to see a doctor."

"Not a chance," I said and waved her off.

She didn't press the issue.

For another three days, I lay in bed, getting up only to eat, shower, and use the bathroom. In all that time I didn't sleep for more than a couple of hours. Sarasi kept insisting I see a doctor, but I refused. My stubbornness and her own lack of sleep made her lose patience with me. After my first night of restlessness and stertorous breathing, she threatened to move to a different room in the house. After the second night, in the wee hours, she got up in a state of exasperation and went to one of the vacant rooms upstairs. After the third night, when morning came and she found me still in bed with no sign of improvement, she suddenly changed her tune.

She sat on the bed next to me and gently pressed various parts of my body. Does it hurt here? Or here? How about here?

As her hands went over me like a professional nurse's, I told her it didn't hurt anywhere in particular, and yet it hurt everywhere, from my glutes to my neck. She didn't like the sound of that. Something would have to be done, she said; she refused to stand by and watch me waste away in bed, potentially for days on end. Was I averse to seeing a doctor?

I wasn't, no, given the circumstances, but before I could tell her this, she disappeared from the room.

She returned a few minutes later with her mother and Nalika in tow. The three of them hovered at the end of my bed like inquisitors. Nalika, it appeared, had been elected spokesperson for the group. She stood a half-step in front of the other two, her arms akimbo. Looking me straight in the eyes, she said, "We think you should see a doctor."

"Okay," I said, upon which the three women exchanged confused glances. Clearly they hadn't expected me to acquiesce so easily, no doubt because Sarasi knew my attitude toward doctors: that I despised them and that if I never saw one again, it would be too soon. But at the moment I didn't feel I had much choice. Something would have to be done, as Sarasi said. Obviously I couldn't stay in bed forever.

Nalika's arms dropped from her hips. "If we could get you an appointment this afternoon, would you go?"

"On one condition," I said.

She smiled indulgently. "Which is?"

I sat up in bed with a herculean effort, trying to give myself some semblance of dignity for what I was about to say. I couldn't very well get onto my soapbox lying down. "No orthopedists," I began, as if "orthopedists" were a dirty word. "I've seen more of them than I can count, and not a single one of them was worth their salt. It was also an orthopedist—the incomparable Dr. Sharp—who convinced me, after only a cursory examination, to have ankle surgery. And look where *that* got me." I paused for a moment, feeling the urge to spit. I had enough vitriol in me to go on for several more minutes, but presently Sarasi gave me a cease-and-desist look. It wasn't the first time she heard me rant about doctors, and she probably suspected that I had only just gotten started. I lay back down, resigned that I had said enough.

Before the three women left my room, they assured me, each in her turn, that I had nothing to worry about on the doctor front, their voices coming at me in a flurry of advice. For her part, Sarasi knew more about my medical history than most of my previous doctors combined, and she had no intention, she said, of sending me to another hands-off practitioner of Western medicine. She had someone else in mind, someone less orthodox, a Dutch physician with a medical doctorate in alternative medicine from India. His name was Dr. Maarten Devos, and, as it happened, he had an office at Lanka Hospital on Baseline Road just minutes from my in-laws'. The moment Sarasi stopped talking, Nalika continued in her stead, as if an invisible baton had been handed off. Dr. Devos was married to a Sri Lankan, whom she, Nalika, knew personally through her veterinary practice, having treated a magnificent ridgeback of theirs named Goliath. And if the husband was anything like the wife, well … What was more (another invisible handoff of the baton), his reputation preceded him, or so my mother-in-law Lalanthi claimed. She informed me rhapsodically that a friend of hers recently went to him with hip trouble and—through a regimen of joint adjustments, physical therapy, and exercise— made a full recovery. She would definitely go to him herself, if and when she ever had similar troubles of her own.

I quietly listened to the praise of Dr. Devos, weighing in my mind everything that was said as well as everything that was not. I had my doubts, to be sure. For instance, there was something dubious to me about Lalanthi's description of her friend's experience, sounding as it did like a religious conversion. This tended to play into my preconceived notions about alternative medicine. Rightly or wrongly, I put Ayurvedic and similar medicines on par with snake charming and astrology; all of these professions relied on the gullibility of their clientele for success. To be fair, Dr. Devos was hardly a snake charmer, and the alternative medicine he practiced seemed to be a cut above the rest. He had medical degrees and worked at a hospital, no less. Also, what did I have to lose? In going to him, I wouldn't be any worse off than I was now. At least I could be sure of one thing about a doctor of alternative medicine: he wasn't likely to recommend surgery as a solution to my back problem.

I agreed to have Nalika make arrangements for me to see Dr. Devos that afternoon, and both she and Sarasi accompanied me. When we arrived at Lanka Hospital for my appointment, we were directed to a check-in counter and waiting room in the basement, which was dark and dreary. It wasn't an auspicious beginning. The one consolation was that we didn't have to wait long. Within five minutes of checking in and filling out some paperwork, my name was called. I was taken aback by this, as I wasn't used to such service. In the States, my average wait time at doctors' offices had been about forty-five minutes. One time, I had to wait for a podiatrist for nearly two hours, an hour in the waiting room and another fifty minutes in the examination room. Then when the doctor finally arrived to exam me, he had the audacity to ask me if I wouldn't mind returning another time. It was nearly five o'clock on a Friday afternoon, he complained, as if that were *my* fault. Could I come back next week?

A Tamil nurse led me to a small examination room where Dr. Devos, or a man in a white lab coat whom I presumed to be Dr. Devos, was already waiting for me. "Andrew, is it?" the man said, reaching out to shake my hand. His accent was so strong, he pronounced the letter "s" in the word "is" like an "s" instead of like a "z." Without a doubt he was Dutch. He must have thought I could infer from his lab coat who he was because he didn't introduce himself.

"Andrew Mauer, yes," I said and shook his hand. As discreetly as I could, I assessed his appearance. He was much older than I expected, not a day under eighty. He had liver-spotted hands, sagging jowls, and the underbite of someone who wore dentures. There was, to me at least, a vast disconnect between the accolades I had heard about him from Lalanthi and what I was seeing of him now. Trying to be cute, I added, "I'm told you know a friend of my mother-in-law's."

Either he didn't hear my comment, or else he ignored it. "Let me see," he said, browsing through my file. "So you're having back problems." His "back" sounded like "beck" as though he were Australian. "Could you remove your shirt, please, and identify where it hurts."

I took off my shirt. "The entirety of my back hurts. But more so my low back. And I'm in pain just standing here."

He appeared to turn this over in his mind. Then he said absently, as if thinking out loud, "Pain is a cry for energy."

I nodded, not having the foggiest idea what he meant. When it came to mysticism and New Age claptrap, I was decidedly ignorant. "I could use some energy," I agreed. "I've had about five hours of sleep in as many days."

Again he didn't respond. Perhaps he was deaf to boot. "Also," he said, picking up where he had left off, "pain is a signal, your body telling you something is wrong." He positioned himself directly behind me. "Now, slowly bend at your waist and touch your toes."

As I did this, my back made a series of cracking sounds, like a firecracker belt going off. It was a familiar sound. Since

I had arrived in Colombo, whenever I was on my feet for more than a few minutes, the slightest forward bend caused my back to go into paroxysms of decrepitude.

Dr. Devos would have had to be stone deaf not to have heard the cracking in my back. But apparently he hadn't because he continued my examination without interruption.

So I mentioned it.

"That would be consistent," he said enigmatically, running a thumb from one vertebra of my spine to the next. He started at the base of my neck and ended at my low back.

"That's where it hurts the most," I said as his hands lingered over my sacrum.

He made an inexplicable grunting noise and mumbled something I could only assume was in Dutch. "As I suspected," he said sibilantly. Seeming to forget himself, his accent momentarily grew stronger, and he replaced his "th's" with "d's." "Give me your hand. Do you feel dose boney protrusions? Dose are your sacroiliac joints, and dey are subluxated. You know dat word?"

It just so happened I did. It was my habit to do research whenever I found my doctors wanting, which was far too often. I was now a walking encyclopedia of arcane medical knowledge. "It means partial dislocation," I said.

"Correct. I am surprised you know that. Most doctors in the West are not aware the SI joints can be partially dislocated. Or they refuse to believe it. They find nothing on an MRI, and so they fail to diagnose." He proceeded to explain the mechanics of SI joints and the functions of the surrounding ligaments. In his professional opinion, I had what the medical community called SI-joint dysfunction, in which the joints moved either too little or too much. He asked if I had ever gone to a chiropractor. I said I hadn't, but again he seemed not to have heard me. He recommended against chiropractic adjustments, he said. "These treatments are too harsh. They can further weaken the ligaments supporting the SI joints. It is like slamming a door too many times. Eventually the hinges become loose, and the door sags, if that is the right word." He advocated instead using a "soft orthopedic manual therapy" to manipulate the SI joints. He told me proudly that he had developed such a treatment himself. "It is a variant of the Dorn therapy. Before you leave today, I will show you how to adjust yourself. This, and targeted exercises, will heal your back."

Whether his therapy was more than quackery, I couldn't tell. What I could tell was that he clearly knew his stuff, or at least he was intimately familiar with the human body. If nothing else, he was the first doctor I had seen in several years who bothered to examine me thoroughly.

A young Tamil man, also wearing a white lab coat, entered the examination room. He was obviously a member of the hospital staff, but it was equally certain that in a different context he could have passed as a teenager.

"This is my assistant," Dr. Devos said, turning to me. "His name is Mathan. Would you mind if he observes me work? He's in training, you see."

I exchanged smiles with Mathan. "Not in the least," I said.

"Very good," said Dr. Devos. "You may put your shirt on. And remove your shoes." He adjusted the examination table, presumably to accommodate my body length, then patted it as an indication for me to lie down.

I removed my shoes and got onto the table.

"On your back, please. Before I check your leg length, is there anything else of importance you would like to tell me about your health?"

I told him about my history of ankle problems, about the difficulty I had had walking and standing, about the botched surgery—and that I had only just gotten over all of that. "I'm at my wits' end," I said. "It's like my body's coming apart at the seams."

He looked at me sympathetically. "Not good," he said. "It might be connected to your back. Everything is connected. Your back, your hips, your knees, your feet." He grabbed my legs at the ankles and lifted them off the table. "Please relax. I am going to check your leg length now. Keep your legs straight but relaxed." He cupped both ankles in one hand and with his free hand gestured for Mathan to come closer to the table. In a teacherly voice, he said, "It is always important to tell your patients what is to follow in order to eliminate anxiety."

Mathan smiled, and Dr. Devos continued with my examination. Still holding my feet by the ankles, he shook my legs as though limbering them up for strenuous exercise, after which he raised them off the table at a 60-degree angle. Then, in a circular motion, he dropped them down to just above the table, separated them in a spread eagle, and brought them back up to where they started, ankle to ankle. He repeated this a few times. With his thumbs on my heels and his fingers around my ankle joints, he looked from my feet to my face. "Your left leg is one centimeter shorter than your right," he said matter-of-factly.

"What does that mean?"

"We will have to adjust your hip joints to realign your legs. And you will have to do this regularly at home." He instructed Mathan to show me how to do the adjustments lying down, both with a hand and a towel. The entire time, Dr. Devos stood to the side and scrutinized our technique. At one point he said, "Be careful not to pull too hard; you don't want to pull your leg off."

I was so confused by it all, and I was so tired because of the lack of sleep, I didn't have the presence of mind to ask what the hips had to do with the back.

Dr. Devos suddenly clapped his hands together. "Off the table, please. I will now demonstrate for you how to self-correct your SI joints."

Mathan helped me off the table.

"Hold onto something for balance," Dr. Devos said. "Like this." He put a hand onto the examination table. "On the side where the SI joint is subluxated, put your fist on the highest point of the *spina iliaca posterior superior*. Right fist for the right side and left fist for the left side. I am assuming my right SI joint is subluxated. So with my right fist positioned here … You see that?"

"Yes."

"While keeping the left foot flat on the floor … like this … and with the knuckles of the right hand firmly pressed against the affected area … like this … you swing the leg of the *same* side that is subluxated. Press your knuckles with slowly increasing strength when the leg swings backward and breathe out while pressing. Like this. Now you try."

I mimicked his movements.

"A little slower. It is not a race. And press and breathe only when the leg swings backward."

I tried it again, this time more slowly and precisely.

"Yes, very good. Now the other side."

I repeated the motions on my left side.

"Good. Do this at home regularly, and do both your left and right sides because both SI joints are subluxated. Keep in mind that these adjustments are only a start. For your SI joints to heal, you will also have to do exercises. After we finish here, Mathan will give you a handout on exercises for the low back and show you proper technique. And before I forget, I will give you this." He handed me a piece of paper. On it was the name of an author and a book—Sarah Key's *Back Sufferers' Bible*— as well as an ISBN. "The book is an excellent resource. It explains in detail how the spine works and shows in words and pictures the proper technique for therapeutic exercises. The ISBN there is for the Indian edition, so you should be able to find a copy locally." He shook my hand. "You will see me again in three days. Until then, do the adjustments and exercises. And, *in godsnaam*, get some sleep."

After my discussion with Mathan, I went to find Sarasi and Nalika in the waiting room. Immediately they started in on me. How did it go? What did Dr. Devos say? Was he able to make a diagnosis? I didn't want to get their hopes up—or mine, for that matter—so I was evasive in answering their questions, saying only that I had been given some exercises to do and that, mainly, we would have to wait and see.

But once we got back to my in-laws', I wasted no time implementing Dr. Devos' therapy. To start with, I asked Nalika to track down the *Back Sufferers' Bible*. She was eager to help, she said. She would try the Vijatha Yapa Bookshop near Majestic City. It had a large selection of textbooks, including medical texts, and she was certain it would have in stock what I was looking for.

Sure enough, an hour later, she returned to the house with the book and delivered it to my room personally. "Look what I found." She waved the book in the air.

I was elated. "You're an angel."

She made as if to set the book down next to me on the mattress but changed her mind. "Wait a second," she said, moving closer to the bed. In the waning afternoon light, she looked like an older, more intense version of Sarasi. "What do I get in return?"

I smiled. "The money for the book?"

"That's a given."

"And my eternal gratitude?"

She didn't laugh. But with a reluctant flick of her wrist, she handed me the book. "I guess I can live with that," she said with a smile, and left.

I rolled over to the window side of the bed and held the book up to the light. It was definitely an Indian edition, as little had been spent on editing or the cover art. The title itself contained a typo, missing an apostrophe at the end of the word "Sufferers." The cover background was a prosaic two-tone in gradations of blue and puke brown. On the blue side stood a white woman in profile, with jet black hair presumably to appeal to the South Asian audience. She wore a white sleeveless dress; her hands were on the small of her back, which was so arched that her breasts stuck out like cones; and her head was tilted skyward, her mouth parted slightly as if gasping in pain. Superimposed on a black band at the bottom of the book was a subtitle in gray lettering that read: "Understanding Is Half the Cure. You Can Treat Your Own Back!"

I cringed when I saw the exclamation point. It suggested laziness or insecurity on the part of the writer rather than strong feeling. What, I wondered, was Ms. Key trying to hide behind the artificial emotion of her exclamation point?

I leafed through the pages. A total of seven chapters, amounting to over two hundred pages. I wouldn't be able to read it all in one go, not with my back the way it was, so I skipped ahead to the last chapter, which was entitled "Treating Your Own Back." Besides not having an exclamation point in its title—itself enough to recommend it—the chapter was chock-full of information on stretching and strengthening exercises, with detailed diagrams and descriptions of proper techniques.

As I lay there planning out my physical-therapy routine, dreading the long road ahead of me, I saw in my mind the legion of doctors I went to during the past ten years. Their ugly faces flitted by as if I were riffling through the pages of a mug book. They were all in an enormous room together—Dr. Sharp, the orthopedic surgeon who operated on my ankle, acting as the ringleader—and they were laughing, sadistically and at my expense. A surge of hatred welled up inside me. *Everything is connected*, Dr. Devos had said. Now I understood what he meant. The feet were connected to the back and vice versa. And ankle surgery could affect—well, it could affect everything. To hell with my former doctors, I thought. I resolved then and there to finish devising an exercise routine and to commence it, with as much energy as I could muster, first thing in the morning, even if it would kill me.

I was jotting down notes from the Key book when Sarasi turned up to tell me dinner was ready.

"I won't be eating," I said bluntly.

She stood on the threshold of the room with her arms crossed. "You can't *not* eat. Ammi has ordered *kothu* roti."

"I'm sorry, but I'm not hungry." Everything—the heat, the sleep deprivation, the anger at my doctors, the anxiety about my back—had conspired to spoil my appetite.

"I wish you had told me sooner."

"It's not like the food will go to waste," I said. "Give my share to the servants."

"That's not the point. It's the principle. Ammi went to the trouble to get *kothu* from Tasty Caterers specially for you because she knows how much you like it."

There was nothing I could say to that. "Fine," I said and grudgingly got out of bed.

In the dining room, my in-laws and Nalika and Sarasi and a man I didn't know were all at the table. I sat down in the empty seat, waiting for someone to introduce me to the man, but no one did.

"What are you waiting for?" Lalanthi said to me. "Here, it's your favorite." She lifted up one of the Styrofoam boxes filled with steaming chicken curry and roti noodles. "Have as much you as like."

I scooped some of the food onto my plate and took a bite. When I looked up again, the mystery man was gone. "Is this someone's idea of a joke?" I asked.

Glances went round the table. The pendant lamp above us flickered.

"What's the matter?" Sarasi asked.

Lalanthi frowned. "You don't like the *kothu*? Is it too spicy?"

"Leave him be," Sunil said. "Can't you see he's not well?"

"It's true," I said. "I'm not feeling well." Somewhere far off, like from a distant planet, the diminished chords of a piano trembled.

Sarasi and Nalika stood up and I felt my eyes go heavy and then everything went dark.

When I came to, I was in bed. I couldn't have been asleep for more than an hour. The lamp on the side table was on. My back was killing me. In exasperation I picked up the Key book and tossed it onto the floor. It landed in such a way that the lamplight made visible the slight discoloration on the book's cover just above the woman's mouth, which now looked like a misty exhalation of breath accompanying her gasp of pain. The sight of this reminded me that I hadn't done any SI-joint adjustments since my visit to Dr. Devos.

I went to the end of the bed and began to swing my leg. Just at that moment Sarasi burst into the room. I almost fell over. "Why don't you knock," I stammered. The adjustment was so kooky-looking I felt like I had just been caught masturbating.

"I shouldn't have to knock on my own room door."

"Technically it's no longer your room because you moved out."

"Don't be a jerk. You know perfectly well why I moved. Anyway, I came to see how you're doing. You passed out, you know. And you were talking in your sleep. Something in German, I think. '*Hau ab, hau ab,*' you kept saying."

"I hope you don't mind if lie down," I said. I sprawled out on the bed with a groan.

"So you're okay?"

"As well as can be expected."

She reached down and picked up the Key book from the floor and set it onto the side table. "We're worried about you," she said.

"Who's *we*?"

"Nalika. Me. Ammi. Thathi. Everyone."

"There's nothing to worry about."

She didn't seem convinced. She raised her eyebrows before leaving the room, and I couldn't blame her. She had every reason to be suspicious of me; I hardly believed myself what I had said. *Hau ab*? Why had I spoken in German? And who was it that I wanted to *go away*?

I performed my ablutions and went to bed. Even before my head hit the pillow, I could tell it was going to be a long night. There was no position—on my back, my stomach, my side— that was comfortable. I rolled around for a couple of hours before falling asleep, only to wake up an hour later. Time dragged on interminably as I tossed and turned.

Around midnight, I gave up trying to sleep. I got dressed and sneaked upstairs to the sitting room. If I couldn't sleep, I thought, I would at least do something constructive. The house was dark, but in the moonlight coming through the French doors of the sitting room, I could see well enough to make out the yoga mat I had previously set up on the area rug. I was just starting my third set of exercises, some leg lifts, when my low back made a popping sound. I lowered my legs onto the mat, afraid to move any more than I had to. For several minutes I lay there, completely motionless, staring up at the ceiling in the dark. What was I going to do? I couldn't sleep. I couldn't do exercises. I couldn't—. I couldn't even think properly to think of what else I couldn't do. The insomnia was driving me mad.

I eased up from the mat. My back didn't seem to be any worse for wear. I groped my way to the side door that led to a second-story staircase and down into the garden.

The air outside was damp and still. The only sounds came from the crickets and from the frogs in the marsh behind the house. On Galpotha Road, no one else was about. I moved fitfully in the anemic light of the streetlamps, the entire time clenching my lower abs like Mathan taught me to do. At a fork in the road, I veered left. I remembered that not far away was a dilapidated colonial bungalow that belonged to a reclusive uncle of Sunil's. When I was level with the bungalow, something possessed me to turn down the lane. The moon shone through the fronds of the palm trees that lined the lane, lighting up my way. As I drew closer to the house, I heard voices. A light was on in one of the rooms. I stopped at the stepping stones that led across a lily pond to the front door. The pale petals of the lilies, like small cupped hands, rose up luminously out of the black water.

The shutters of the living room were open. I could hear the voices more clearly now. There were two of them: one the high-pitched cadences of a Sri Lankan; the other, the mountain twang of an American. They spoke urgently. Their silhouettes moved back and forth across the room. Shadows played on the interior walls.

I stepped onto the first of the stones. It shifted under my weight and sent a ripple of water through the pond. I stood still. Above the moon and the canopy of stars, a three-note ostinato swayed to the rhythm of the lily pads' rise and fall.

A figure appeared in the window—a white man. He looked out into the moonlit night, his hair hanging down to his shoulders in disheveled gray strands. He was the same man, I realized, I had seen at dinner.

I fell back onto the path of the loggia, kicking up gravel.

Another figure appeared in the window. "Who's there?" a voice called out in Sinhala.

Before I knew what I was doing, I said "Go away" and turned and ran. Within seconds, I was back on the street, doubled over, catching my breath. I couldn't feel my legs. I stood upright, panting, and looked in the direction of the bungalow. No one appeared to be following me. I shouldn't have come, I thought. I had been a fool, a damned fool. What if something had happened? Out in the middle of the night, alone. As quickly I could, I limped back to my in-laws'. The road was as devoid of life as it had been before.

I got to my room and fell into bed with my clothes on. A swath of moonlight, which was coming through the window, cast an elongated grillwork shadow on the opposite wall. I positioned myself on my back, with perfect posture, and clenched my abs to the point of hurting. After several minutes of lying perfectly still, a rush of adrenaline went up my vagus nerve, followed by a tingling sensation in the brain. My stomach contracted, and then a jolt of electricity ran down my left shoulder and arm. I twitched from the aftershock. My heart began to pound. I was perspiring so profusely, the bed sheets were soaked. I seemed to be on the verge of passing out. Alternately my bladder and bowels loosened, like a pendulum, as though my center of gravity were shifting. For a split second I thought I could feel the workings of my internal organs.

I un-tensed my body and slackened my posture. Instantly a sense of release overcame me. My stomach expanded. As I drifted off to sleep, a hint of lemon permeated the back of my mouth.

I awoke two hours later with the rising sun. A koel was screaming in the breadfruit tree outside my window. I went to the kitchen.

Sunil was making tea. "Good morning," he said, setting down the electric kettle. "Did you sleep well?"

"It was the most sleep I've had in six days." I put my hands on my low back. There was only a slight ache. "I feel like I could run a marathon."

"That may be premature." He looked me up and down. "But I grant you, you do look better."

I wanted to tell him what I had seen earlier at his uncle's bungalow, but something, a voice deep in the recesses of my mind, prevented me.

"Would you like a cup of tea?"

"No, thanks," I said. "I have exercises to do."

In the sitting room, my yoga mat was where I had left it. One by one I did the exercises I mapped out the day before. None of them caused my back to worsen, and, if anything, they made it feel more limber. I had to tell someone the good news.

I dashed to Sarasi's room. She was still in bed. "Sarasi, wake up," I said. I sat down next to her and shaded my eyes from the light that was pouring through the half-open shades. "It's a miracle."

"What's a miracle? What are you talking about?" As she sat up, her hair fell down over her face.

"My back. It's getting better."

She brushed the hair from her eyes and tucked it behind her ears. "Are you sure? Only yesterday—"

"I've never been more sure of anything in my life."

"Does that mean you slept through the night?"

"Well, not exactly."

"What do you mean *not exactly*? Either you did, or you

didn't."

"I didn't. But I think I got a total of four hours' sleep."

Nalika came into the room. "What's going on?"

"What is this, Union Station?" Sarasi said. "Could I have some privacy, please?"

"Oh, come on, Sarasi," said Nalika, "it's not like I haven't seen you in a tank top and underwear before." She sat on the end of the bed in the lotus position, looking from Sarasi to me and back again. "You didn't answer my question."

"Andrew says he slept for four hours last night and is feeling better."

"That's wonderful. We should celebrate."

Sarasi made a face.

"*Or*," Nalika said and slid off the bed and hurried from the room.

She returned a minute later with a photograph. To me she said, "I wasn't going to mention this because of everything that was happening with your back, but we've been invited to a wedding." She handed me the photograph. "Her name is Anjali. She's a friend of mine from Visakha. Originally she had only invited me and Ammi and Thathi. But when she found out Sarasi was in town, she invited the two of you as well." She tapped the photograph. "That's her fiancé Jack. He's Australian."

I cringed. "He has sideburns. Why does he have sideburns?"

"I don't know," Nalika said. "They've come back into fashion?"

"No, they haven't."

"What does it matter?"

"Andrew hates sideburns," Sarasi said.

"All you have to do is attend the wedding," said Nalika. "You don't have to approve of the fiancé."

"When is it?" I handed back the photograph.

"Two days from now."

"I'll go," I said.

Sarasi touched my hand. "You're sure you'll be okay? I don't want you to do anything to aggravate your back."

"Everything will be fine." I leaned over and closed the shades, darkening the room.

A little later, in my own room, I tried to nap, but I couldn't sleep. It was too hot and humid, and the birds in the garden were too loud. So I tracked down Lalanthi and asked if she would mind taking me to the Sinhalese Sports Club for a swim.

"I'd be happy to," she said.

I gathered up my swim stuff in a tote bag, and we drove over to Maitland Place.

At the entrance to SSC, Lalanthi checked me in and paid the two-hundred-rupee guest fee. "I'll be back in an hour to pick you up," she said.

I went through the turnstile, past the pool, and to the men's dressing room. An attendant at the door took my name down in a registry. When he heard my accent, he asked, "Are you American?"

I said I was.

He had a confused look on his face. "Mauer is an American name?"

"It's German. It means 'wall'—as in, you give me enough space and time and I can see through a brick wall."

He looked even more confused.

In the dressing room behind him, an elderly Sri Lankan and a white man, who I later determined was an Englishman, were stepping out of their clothes and into their swimsuits. The Englishman must have been eavesdropping on my conversation with the attendant. "Bloody Americans," I heard him say as I walked in.

"Excuse me?" I said.

"A bunch of arrogant bastards, if you ask me." He didn't seem to be talking to anyone in particular. Since I had entered the room, he hadn't so much as acknowledged me, not even after I stood in front of him.

Meanwhile the elderly Sri Lankan man disappeared into the showers and the dressing-room attendant abandoned his post.

I was about to tell the Englishman to mind his own business when he looked at me and said, "No need to get your knickers in a twist, mate." He snapped the elastic of his Speedo around his flabby midsection and, without showering, went to the pool.

I changed into my swimsuit, showered, and followed the Englishman out. The only available lane in the pool was next to him. I removed my flip-flops and washed my feet in one of the poolside basins and got into the lane. For some reason the Englishman wasn't swimming; he was just floating on his back, his paunch jutting into the air. As I stretched and put on my goggles, I glanced in the direction of the front desk. The dressing-room attendant was there talking to one of the clerks, gesturing toward me and the Englishman. Whatever I was going to do, I thought, it would have to be discreet.

A murder of crows was roosting in a flame tree between the front desk and the pool. One of them cawed now, then swooped down and foraged in the grass.

I swam the breaststroke for three-quarters of a mile. Each time I passed the Englishman in the water, I tried not to look at him. When I finished my swim and got out of the pool, he was still floating in his lane as I hoped he would be. Dripping wet, I made my way to the dressing room as fast as my flip-flops would allow me. The attendant was gone, and no one was in the dressing room. I dried off hurriedly and threw on my clothes without showering. Then I picked up the Englishman's clothes and took them to one of the bathroom stalls. A turd was floating in the toilet. "For Queen and country," I said, and dropped the clothes and flushed.

Moments later, I was out front of SSC waving down Lalanthi.

"How was it?" she asked as I got into the car.

"Extremely satisfying."

I wasn't hungry when we got home, so I skipped lunch. I read another chapter of the *Back Sufferers' Bible*, did a few hip- and SI-joint adjustments, and then went upstairs to the sitting room to exercise again. Nalika and Sunil were there, on the planter's chairs, having tea and watching a cricket match.

"Where are Sarasi and Lalanthi?" I asked.

"They're out shopping for Anjali's wedding," Nalika said.

"You don't mind if I do some exercises, do you?"

"Please do," Sunil said, motioning to the floor.

I lay down on my yoga mat. I started off with a piriformis stretch, then the puppy and sphinx poses. After a set each of partial crunches and reverse curl ups, I rolled over onto my stomach to alleviate the pressure on my back. As I did so, I saw something flit across the tapestry on the wall above the daybed. I sat up. "Did you see that?"

The crowd on the TV erupted in applause.

"I know, I know." Sunil joined the applause. "It sailed clear over the long boundary. A monster of a shot."

A draft came through the French doors and stirred the tapestry. The Sigiriya women depicted on it heaved a sigh. Who they once were, the life of objectification they once led, communicated itself to me through the ages in the three-circled tattoos around their necks.

"Is something the matter?" Sunil asked me.

"No, nothing's the matter," I said. I turned away to hide the tears in my eyes. "I think I just need some food. I'm absolutely starving. Are there any leftovers from lunch?"

"I'll help you find something," Nalika said.

We went downstairs to the kitchen.

"Really," I said as Nalika pulled various containers from the refrigerator and set them onto the counter, "you don't need to trouble yourself. I'm perfectly capable—"

"Oh, it's no trouble. Let's see, we had string hoppers and egg curry for lunch, so there's that, and there's the leftover *kothu* from last night, and then two days ago we had *godamba* roti. Which would you like?"

"The hoppers sound good."

She heated up a plate of food for me in the microwave and said, "I'll keep you company while you eat."

I turned on the ceiling fan, and we sat down at the kitchen table.

"Did Sarasi say how long she'd be gone?" I asked between bites.

"She should be home any time now," Nalika said. She got up and poured me a glass of water and sat back down. "Are you sure you're all right? Your eyes are bloodshot."

"I didn't sleep well again last night." As I took a sip of water, the image of the gray-haired American flashed through my mind. I had almost forgotten about him. It all seemed so long ago. "And then I couldn't nap earlier. I have this boundless energy that nothing seems to satisfy."

"The swim this morning didn't help?"

"It did, but not in the way I expected."

"I have an idea." She folded her hands on the table. "You and Sarasi and I should go to a club tonight. There's a new one on Horton Place called The Royal Burgh. It's owned by a retired Scottish couple. We could go there and get your mind off things. You might be able to sleep afterward too."

Sarasi entered the kitchen. "I'm so glad you're eating," she said to me, setting her shopping bags onto the table. "I'm not interrupting anything, am I?"

"Nalika thinks we should go to a club tonight," I said. I leaned back in my chair. My entire back was aching.

Nalika pulled one of the bags toward her and rifled through it.

"Maybe that's what you need to help you sleep," Sarasi said. "Forcing yourself to stay up late."

"That's what *I* said." Nalika pulled from the bag a lime-green dress and ran her hand along the fabric. "Is this what you're wearing to the wedding? It's beautiful."

"It looks even better on," said Sarasi. "Do you want to see?"

"Yes, please," Nalika said.

Sarasi swooped up the dress and left the room.

I took my dirty dishes to the sink. A rectangle of sunlight suffused the backsplash, causing the glass tiles to iridescence. Time seemed to stand still as I rinsed off my dishes and stared at the light. The fan whirred overhead. I was reminded of the tapestry, of the Sigiriya women. Those poor women. What did they do to deserve such a fate? And what gave others the right to impose their wills? Throughout the course of history, human nature hadn't changed. People always had been, and always would be, self-serving. The thought weighed heavily on my mind.

An egret squawked somewhere out in the marsh. I finished washing my dishes and placed them onto the drying rack.

"Well?" Sarasi twirled into the room with her new dress on.

"It goes perfectly with your skin," said Nalika.

"Careful," I said. "You don't want to show up the bride."

Sarasi kissed me. "You're not so bad-looking yourself," she whispered.

I held her in my arms for a moment. "That reminds me. What am I going to wear to the wedding myself? I don't even have a suit."

"I've already thought of that," she said. "You have an appointment tomorrow morning with Thathi's tailor, Mr. Amerasinghe. I hope you don't mind wearing an Indian sherwani, though. It was all Ammi and I could find at such short notice."

"As long as it's not one of those silk embroidered ones."

Nalika laughed. "You mean you don't want to look like a Bollywood star?"

"I'm more worried about looking like a clown."

"We bought a plain black one," Sarasi said. "It's in the other bag if you want to look at it."

I opened the bag. The sherwani was indeed black and unadorned. In fact, it looked more like a British frock coat than Indian formalwear. "That'll do."

"By the way," Nalika said, "we still haven't figured out our plans for tonight. So what do you think? Shall we go to a club?"

"It's up to Andrew," said Sarasi. "He's the one suffering from insomnia."

The ache in my back was spreading upward. "I'll think about it," I said, rubbing the nape of my neck.

For the rest of the afternoon, the hours blurred one into the other. I tried to nap again but without success. The temperature was getting hotter—the weather was about to break, Sunil said, triggering the southwest monsoon. To stay cool, I went about the house wearing only a sarong and flip-flops. The idea of spending the night at a club instead of rolling around in a pool of sweat for several hours was looking increasingly attractive.

At dinner Nalika asked me what I had decided about going out.

"You don't have to twist my arm," I said. "The nightclub it is."

The Royal Burgh was in the Kurunduwatta District. Its faux

brick façade looked like a Shakespearean stage set. Balconies flanked its front entrance, and a balustrade ran the length of its roof, like the parapet of a castle.

When Sarasi, Nalika, and I arrived at a little past ten, we were given the last of the club's available tables. The whole place was alive with activity. Sri Lankans and Westerners alike packed the dance floor. As we entered, they were dancing to a Joseph K song, "It's Kinda Funny," that was playing dissonantly on the jukebox. In the blue strobe lights, the dancers' gyrating bodies moved in slow motion.

A waitress came by and took our drink orders. No sooner had she done so than the air-conditioner broke. We looked on in disbelief as club staff went around flinging open windows and doors, strategically placing floor fans, and lighting citronella-oil lamps. Almost instantly my kurta and jeans were sticking to my body.

"Not a word!" Nalika said above the music before I could complain.

The Cure song "Lullaby" started to play on the jukebox. Robert Smith's silky voice filled the club with whispered menace.

I leaned in so that I could be heard. "At least the music is good. I'd like to check out the jukebox. If I'm going to sweat anyway, I might as well dance. But nothing too fast. I don't want to re-injure my back." I rummaged through Sarasi's purse until I found some rupee coins and then headed for the jukebox.

It stood to one side of the dance floor. A thirty-something European-looking guy was already there, in the midst of making a selection. I looked at the music over his shoulder while I waited. It was mostly vintage British bands, a mix of post-punk, synth-pop, and Gothic rock. I recognized only a few slow songs, one of which was "Wraith" by the Scottish band The Thanes.

The European-looking guy pressed a button on the jukebox and turned around abruptly. "Sorry, mate," he said as he stepped on my foot. He wasn't European but Australian. Before I could say anything, he scurried off to his table. There was something familiar about him, but I couldn't quite place it.

To the sound of the opening bass riff of the Talking Heads' "Psycho Killer," I inserted a coin into the jukebox and selected "Wraith."

"Did you find anything decent?" Sarasi asked when I got back to our table.

"Yes, but it's going to be awhile before it plays. There are about ten other songs in the queue." My beer, a Scottish ale called Witch's Brew, was waiting for me on the table. I took a sip. It tasted of toasted malts and dried fruit, with a bite of habanero chili. I set down my glass, noticing as I did so that Nalika was gone. "Where's Nalika?"

"Someone asked her to dance."

Forty-five minutes later, the song I had selected from the jukebox came on. It opened with an achingly melancholy cello and violin duet.

"This is it." I took Sarasi by the hand. She looked ravishing in her black sleeveless dress. Even from a distance, I could smell the jasmine in her hair.

We passed Nalika on the way to the dance floor. She stopped us. "You won't believe who I just saw," she said.

Sarasi let go of my hand. "Who?"

"Anjali's fiancé Jack. And he's here with another woman."

"What do you mean *another woman*?" Sarasi asked.

"I mean a woman he's dancing and flirting with who isn't Anjali. If you don't believe me, see for yourself." She pointed at a table near the entrance. A young Sri Lankan woman sat with a blond-haired white man, who had his back to us. Their hands were all over each other. For a moment the man turned in his chair and looked in the direction of the dance floor. It was the Australian who stepped on my foot. Then I recognized him, the guy from the photograph Nalika had shown me.

"What are you going to do?" Sarasi asked.

"What *can* I do? I can't tell Anjali. Her wedding is less than two days away, and it would break her heart."

The Thanes song had reached the eerie tremolos of its keyboard solo, the first in a series of descents into Gothic gloom.

I clenched my abs. "The guy's an asshole," I said. "And he has sideburns. And he stepped on my foot. That's three marks against him."

"He stepped on your foot?" Sarasi said.

"At the jukebox. It was an accident, but still, the guy's an asshole." I took her by the hand again. "Let's dance. The song is almost over."

"It's the Jacks of the world who make me grateful to have someone like you," Sarasi said.

One corner of the dance floor was free. I led Sarasi there. Arm in arm, we swayed to the music. The Thanes' lead singer Duncan Ross, after an orchestral interlude, crooned the last minute of the song to hypnotic electronic beats that would have made stones move. I felt my knees go weak.

Sarasi kissed me at the song's end. "That was wonderful," she said. "When was the last time we danced?"

"Not since our wedding."

"Can we do it again?"

I looked over at the jukebox. The queue was several people long. "Once the line dies down," I said, "I'll pick another slow song."

In our absence, two other women, both in their early to mid-thirties, had joined Nalika at our table. The three of them were having a heated discussion as Sarasi and I sat down.

Nalika gave us a conspiratorial smile. "Sarasi, Andrew, meet Lakshani and Ravima, girlfriends of mine. Lakshani, Ravima, meet my sister Sarasi and my brother-in-law Andrew."

After shaking hands and exchanging pleasantries, with The Clash's "Straight to Hell" playing in the background, I said, "You looked like you were plotting something earlier."

"We were talking about Anjali," Nalika said. She re-capped the discussion she had had with Lakshani and Ravima: that they basically concluded not to say anything to Anjali. The woman with Jack was an old flame of his, and for all Nalika and Lakshani and Ravima knew, Jack and his ex were simply saying a proper goodbye for old time's sake. Other than dancing and putting their hands on each other, Jack hadn't actually done anything objectionable that the three women could see. So why create strife between him and Anjali unnecessarily?

"I could find out for you if anything more is going on," I offered.

Nalika moved forward in her seat. "You mean like spying?"

"I guess. He doesn't know who I am, and so I could introduce myself and probe a little."

"I don't think that's a good idea," Sarasi said.

"How would you introduce yourself?" Nalika asked.

"Leave it to me." I stood up. "I'm going to the jukebox." I could hear Sarasi arguing with Nalika as I walked away.

No one was at the jukebox. I dropped in a coin and selected David Bowie's "The Man Who Sold the World." The dance floor was still jammed with people, moving to the portentous bass pattern of "The Killing Moon."

The moment I got back to our table, more drinks arrived. Nalika and Sarasi had stopped arguing; they were talking and laughing now with Lakshani and Ravima. As the waitress was leaving, I slipped her a thousand-rupee tip when no one else was looking.

I raised my beer glass. "To the general joy of the table. And to Jack. May he deserve what he gets, and may he get what he deserves."

Everyone laughed except Sarasi, who shushed me.

I sat back and looked around the club. The dancing hadn't let up. Those who weren't on the dance floor were at their tables drinking and talking. I didn't see Jack anywhere, or his girlfriend, not at his table or on the dance floor. Maybe he left? If he had, it would be unfortunate because I hadn't had a chance to introduce myself. But maybe he hadn't left. Maybe he was in the bathroom. I excused myself from the table to have a look.

There was a line in front of the men's room. Jack wasn't in it.

"I just have to wash my hands," I said and skipped the line and opened the men's room door and went inside.

All the urinals and stalls were in use. Someone was at one of the sinks. From behind, I could tell it was Jack. His spiked blond hair looked like a crown.

I washed my hands in the sink next to him, looking at my reflection in the mirror. I hardly recognized myself. Jack was looking in the mirror, too. For an instant our eyes met, mirror to mirror, and his face flickered. The head of an old man with long gray hair flashed in place of Jack's.

"Is that your girlfriend you're with?" I asked.

Jack gave me a vacant stare. "I reckon she is," he said, slurring his words. "For the night anyway. Not bad, eh?"

"Not bad at all," I said. "She's almost as attractive as your fiancée."

In the silence that followed, a toilet and a couple of urinals flushed. The men's room door opened and closed, and the refrain "hang the DJ" flooded in.

"Do I know you?" Jack said, a touch of panic in his voice.

I laughed. "No, but you will soon." I left him standing there in a drunken stupor.

"Where have you been?" Sarasi asked me back at our table.

"Taking care of business in the men's room."

"I hope you didn't 'introduce' yourself to anyone."

"I hope you did," Nalika said.

Sarasi gave Nalika the evil eye.

I feigned incredulity. "What, in the bathroom?" Out of the corner of my eye I saw Jack return to his table, hurriedly settle his bill, and then grab his girlfriend's hand and head for the door. His face appeared ashen in the half-light.

The music continued to blare, the strobe lights to flash. A fan was blowing in my face. Across from me, Lakshani and Ravima looked like twins. Their hair was in the same high ponytail, they both had similarly round faces, and they both wore chokers around their necks. Were they, too, someone's object of desire, to be used and discarded at will?

I felt myself starting to flag. I closed my eyes.

I awoke to Sarasi's face in mine. "How long have I been asleep?" I asked.

"A few minutes. You looked so cute, I didn't want to wake you. But I think your song is coming up. Shall we dance and then go home?"

"Okay."

Even before it began to play, the Bowie song ran through my head—*Oh no, not me*—its riff as simple as rainwater yet spellbinding. I led Sarasi to the dance floor again, and again we swayed to the music. Every time the line "You're face to face" came up, we drew closer to each other and sang along.

It was one o'clock by the time we got home. I showered and

went to bed. But the short nap at the club had given me a second wind, so I couldn't sleep. For three hours I lay on my back, stared at the moonlight and listened to the hum of the ceiling fan, until the koel started in as usual outside my window.

I made a cup of coffee in the kitchen and took it up to the sitting room to drink while I exercised and watched the news. There was an interesting segment on BBC about Sylvia Plath and her last days in London: her distress over her husband, the difficulties with the au pair, her erratic behavior, the pills she took to help her sleep at night and the ones she took to get her through the day. I glommed on to the bit about the pills. That was one thing I hadn't tried. I hated drugs almost as much as I hated doctors, but artificial sleep would be better than none. All I needed to figure out was a way to get to the pharmacy.

Sunil and Lalanthi happened to be coming up the stairs with their morning tea. I broached the subject of sleeping pills as they sat down to watch the news.

"We can stop off at Union Chemists on our way back from the tailor's," Lalanthi said. "I can also take you to SSC later today if you like. You said yesterday that it helped your back."

"That's probably not a good idea," I said.

"Why not?"

"What I meant was, my back is doing so much better, it's unnecessary for me to swim. In fact, other than the splitting headache I have right now, I haven't felt this well in days. I'm thinking I might even cancel my follow-up appointment with Dr. Devos."

"Is that wise?" Sunil said.

"I don't want to waste the man's time. Or my own. But I also don't want him to think I'm ungrateful. The man's a prince, and he deserves to be treated like one. Could one of you do me a favor? Could you buy Dr. Devos a gift card and have it delivered to the hospital for me? I'm thinking Rs. 50,000 at that Italian place Sarasi and I went to the last time we were here. What's it called again?"

"Dolce Italia, in Bambalapitiya," Lalanthi said.

"That's the place. Dr. Devos could take his wife there for a nice meal, drink a little wine." Just the thought of the two of them dining together, by candlelight with a bottle of red wine on their table, was enough to alleviate my headache.

Lalanthi and Sunil glanced at each other. "We'll see what we can do," they said in unison.

Four hours later, I was still glowing at the thought of treating Dr. Devos to dinner. I didn't even mind that Mr. Amerasinghe's tailor shop was a poorly ventilated hole in the wall on a dumpy part of Front Street. Literally, a pile of garbage two feet high and twelve feet in diameter was less than half a block from the shop door. I had to hold my breath as Lalanthi, Sarasi, and I walked by.

Mr. Amerasinghe was a long-time friend of Lalanthi's family. He had tailored her father's suits as a young apprentice. He must have been in his seventies by now, but he was still going strong. He carried himself like an old-school British tailor, even dressing the part. He wore a white oxford shirt and a suit vest and hung a tape measure around his neck like a scarf.

I stepped onto a wooden platform in front of a three-panel mirror at the back of the shop. Mr. Amerasinghe stood to one side of me, his head level with my stomach, and assessed my clothes. The sherwani I had just put on was so long, it came down to my thighs, and the churidar pants bunched up at my ankles like a pair of pajamas. Lalanthi and Sarasi had been silent from the moment I came out of the dressing room. They probably expected me to protest, but actually, I was fine with how I looked. I hadn't shaved in over a week, and my facial hair along with my attire made me look like a Mughal prince.

A turban on my head and a pair of juttis on my feet were all I needed to complete the ensemble.

Sarasi cleared her throat. "Well," she said from the couch she and Lalanthi were sitting on, "what do you think?"

"I love it," I said. "Except maybe the pants could be hemmed a little to get rid of some of the excess fabric?"

"Yes, of course, sir," Mr. Amerasinghe said. He folded up each pant leg an inch or two, pinned both sides into place, and made a chalk mark at the bottom of the new hems. "More the American style, no, without the tapering?"

I said it was, yes.

He moved behind me and tugged on the back of my sherwani and ran his hands under my armpits. As he worked, he hummed a melody that was as familiar to me as the rhythms of my own pulse. In an instant everything around me, all the pain and suffering and shabbiness and human want, fell away. I was transported to a flower-strewn meadow amid birdsong and murmuring streams and caressing breezes. The sweet sounds of stringed instruments and a harpsichord floated on the air. Briefly, very briefly, dark figures stirred in the background. Tremolos and arpeggios mimicked thunder and lightning. Then the soft whisperings returned. Out of the storm, a single viola barked, like a dog awakening from a dream.

"That's Vivaldi," I said.

"Is it?" said Mr. Amerasinghe, his head appearing in the mirror from behind me. "I don't know the names of the songs, only the sounds."

"His daughter's a concert violinist," Lalanthi said. "She studied at Juilliard."

My pulse quickened. "Any friend of classical music is a friend of mine."

Mr. Amerasinghe smiled modestly. "I don't get to hear my daughter play her violin live much anymore. Only on the rare occasions she visits Colombo. I'm forced to settle for the recordings she sends me. Vivaldi, did you say?"

The bell above the front door tinkled, and a customer entered the shop.

"Excuse me," Mr. Amerasinghe said. He went to the counter to confer with the customer. A couple of minutes later he came back and said, "Now, where were we? Ah, yes, the cuffs." He positioned himself in front of me. "Please straighten your arms at your sides."

I straightened my arms.

One at a time he grasped the sleeves of my sherwani and deftly pinned and chalked the cuffs. Then he stepped back to within inches of the mirror and examined the fit of my clothes. "Very handsome," he said. "But you are too thin, Mr. Mauer. Before the alterations, the coat hung on you like a gunny bag." He looked at Sarasi. "Do you not feed him, *putā*?"

"He won't eat," Lalanthi chimed in, as if to defend her honor. "We plan meals specially for him, but he won't eat. And when he does, he eats like a bird."

"He's the same at home," Sarasi added.

With the back of a hand, Mr. Amerasinghe swept some chalk from one of my sleeves. "There's a word in English for someone as thin as you, Mr. Mauer. It means ghostly thin. But my memory—it isn't what it used to be."

"You mean *wraith*?" I asked.

He waggled his head. "Yes. Thank you. You are as thin as a wraith."

"I'll take that as a compliment."

While I changed back into my street clothes, Lalanthi and Mr. Amerasinghe conversed outside my dressing-room door. She was concerned, she said, about his having to do alterations in half a day. He was a busy man. Was he sure it wasn't too much trouble? He pooh-poohed her concern. It was no trouble, he said, no trouble at all. The Wijeratne family had been very good to him over the years. How could he ever repay their kindness in helping send his daughter to study in America? Her music was what it was today because of them. So the alterations were no trouble, no trouble at all.

I opened the dressing-room door and handed Mr. Amerasinghe my coat and pants to be altered.

It wasn't until the bell tinkled and the front door closed behind Lalanthi and Sarasi and me that I heard Mr. Amerasinghe yell "Sir!" as if I had forgotten something. He must have found the 5,000-rupee note I tucked into the breast pocket of my sherwani like a kerchief.

"Was that Mr. Amerasinghe calling?" Lalanthi asked.

"It's nothing," I said, and kept right on walking down Front Street.

Outside, it was drizzling. For the two blocks back to the car, Lalanthi and Sarasi shared a parasol while I looked up at the sky and happily let the rain dampen my face and hair.

We took the scenic route over to the pharmacy, past Galle Face Hotel and the sea. Every once in a while, when buildings weren't obstructing my view, I could see the rough, pre-storm surf crashing against the shore. There was something musical about it, like the impassioned movement of a conductor's baton. As if in time to the waves, the windshield wipers of Lalanthi's car swept back and forth, ending each quarter-circle rotation with a metronomic thud.

The pharmacy was on Bagatalle Road. Lalanthi pulled her car up in front of the shop and let the engine idle. "They know you're coming," she said to me.

"Hurry back," Sarasi said. "I'm tired and plan to have a nap when we get home."

Pizzicato raindrops strummed the sidewalk as I stepped from the car. An elderly Sri Lankan woman appeared out of nowhere and silently thrust a hand into my face. She looked like a witch, what with the rags she wore and the ratty hair and the smudges of dirt everywhere.

I felt a tug on my heartstrings. I took all the rupee coins I had in my pockets and poured them into her hand and watched her eyes light up. "My wife and I have so much," I said.

She folded her hands, with the coins clasped between them, and blessed me in Sinhala.

Afterward, in the pharmacy, I was as light as air. Some customers sat in the waiting area, but no one stood at the pickup counter. I walked up to the pharmacist at the window and slid my driver's license onto the deal tray. "I'm here for some zolpidem," I said. "The Mauer order. I believe Dr. Devos phoned it in."

"One moment, please," the pharmacist said in stilted English. He disappeared behind some shelves.

Music was playing over the PA system. I thought I heard the trill of a piano, but the volume was so low, the piece was barely audible.

The pharmacist returned with my sleeping pills and rang up the order.

"Is that '*Für Elise*' you're playing?" I looked up at the speakers on the wall.

He tittered and waggled his head, but clearly he hadn't understood me because nothing about Beethoven was laughable.

I counted out several rupee notes on the tray, more than enough to pay for my pills, and told the pharmacist with a blissful smile to keep the change.

On the drive home, it started raining more heavily. It continued to rain all day. Little by little it turned into a steady downpour. By evening, black sheets blotted out the sky. Thunder cracked overhead. The gutters of my in-laws' house overflowed so much that water cascaded off the roof. Standing at a window inside the house was like standing in a cave behind a waterfall.

I was exhausted at day's end. After dinner, I took a couple of sleeping pills and turned in early. I fell asleep almost immediately, to the ambient, white-noise sound of rain. In my dreams I saw myself floating face down in the sea, being battered by the waves. I was miles and miles away from shore. Heavy drops of ice-cold water fell in a regular rhythm on my back and head. Then suddenly a dazzling light filled the sky and the wind and rain became a cataclysm, a universal deluge, the end of the world.

I woke up in a sweat. It wasn't raining anymore. The power had gone out, and the ceiling fan was dead. An oppressive closeness pervaded the room.

Guided only by the moon, I got out of bed and felt my way to the kitchen. I poured myself some water from the clay dispenser. Then I poured another glass and drank it, and then another. Something inside me was insatiable. I grabbed a bunch of plantains and sat down at the table and ate every last one of them.

I heard a noise come from upstairs. I sat utterly still, holding my breath and clenching my abs.

"Who's there?" someone called from the bottom of the staircase. Seconds later a human form appeared in the doorway to the kitchen. From the white tank top, I could see that it was Sarasi.

"Jesus." I strained my eyes in the dark to see her face. "You scared me."

"Andrew?" she said. "What are you doing?"

"Getting some water." I pushed the plantain peels onto the floor.

"Why are you sitting in the dark?"

"The sleeping pills didn't work. What time is it?"

"Half past ten."

"Shit. The night's only begun." I unclenched my abs. My appetite had gone.

She pulled up a chair at the table. I could sense what was coming. "You've been acting strangely, Andrew. Everyone says so. Even Thathi, who's normally very tolerant of eccentricity ..." She paused, and in the silence, a lone dog barked in the distance.

"Did you hear that?" I asked.

"Hear what?"

"The dog."

An eternity seemed to pass as we stared at each other in the dark.

At last she choked back a sob, wiped a hand across her face. "I don't know what to do," she said.

My patience was running thin. I just wanted to be left alone. "There's nothing to do. Seriously, everything's fine. I told you, I was thirsty, is all."

I didn't hear her get up from the chair, or her footsteps as she went back upstairs. Nor did I hear my own footsteps as I, too, went back to bed.

The power had been restored. In my room the ceiling fan was humming again. I lay in bed, unable to sleep, and I had the feeling that this exact sequence of events had happened before, not just the lying in bed in a pool of sweat and the moonlight streaming through the window and the hum of the ceiling fan, but also the conversation with Sarasi and making her cry and wanting to be left alone. At the same time, a half-remembered song surfaced from the depths of my memory. I began to lip sync fragments of the lyrics. Of their own volition my arms carved the air. A hand clamped shut like the jaws of a crocodile. An index finger shot out. I raised my upper torso, held it like a crunch, let it fall back again. My energy was spent. Hour after hour after hour I lay there—immobile, eyes wide open—the melody of the song echoing in my mind.

I crawled out of bed as soon as the koel began its morning routine. I was delirious. Others of the household were already stirring upstairs. Between the raucous birdcalls, I heard a murmur of voices.

I found everyone gathered in the sitting room: Nalika and Sarasi on the daybed; Sunil and Lalanthi on the planter's chairs. They went quiet the moment they saw me.

"Don't mind me," I said. "I just came to do some exercises." I sat down on the yoga mat and positioned myself in a half-lotus.

"We were planning out the logistics of getting to the wedding this evening," said Sunil.

"Sure you were," I said.

There was an awkward silence. Everyone had serious expressions on their faces. My head felt like it was about to explode.

"We might as well tell him," Nalika said finally. She put an arm around Sarasi's shoulders.

"Tell me what?" I said, switching my legs.

As Sarasi spoke, my ears started to ring, and I couldn't understand a word she was saying. I stared at her moving lips, at the dark, lunate patches under her eyes. Again I switched my legs. Through the ringing, I caught only snatches of sentences, something about her wanting me to see a doctor. It wasn't healthy to go days with little or no sleep, she said, and the doctor she wanted me to see could help with that, too. There was no shame in it. He had treated some of the finest minds in Colombo.

I tried to interject something, to say I had had my fill of doctors, but the words wouldn't come out.

Then the ringing stopped. Nalika's voice rose above the clamor in my head. "We all think it would be best," she said, "if you didn't attend the wedding. Thathi has agreed to stay home and look after you."

"But I don't need looking after," I managed to stammer.

"Stop pretending everything's fine," Sarasi said suddenly, on the verge of tears. "It's not fine, and you know it isn't. You're seeing things. You're hearing things."

"I don't know what you're talking about." I moved my fingers as if plucking the strings of a violin.

Sarasi glowered at me. "Ammi got a phone call last night from a friend of hers who's a member at SSC. Do you know what she said?"

A vague image came to me amid a jumble of other thoughts, of a set of clothes swirling around in a shit-caked toilet bowl. "I think I can guess."

"Come now, children," Sunil interrupted. "Arguing won't help anything."

I sighed a sigh of the resigned. "Do what you will," I said. "I don't have the energy to resist."

Lalanthi leaned forward in her chair and touched my face. "We only want what's best for you, dear."

House arrest, it seemed, was what was best for me.

Later that day, Sunil carried out his duties as if his life depended on it. Except when I was in bed or in the bathroom, he followed me around like my personal valet. I knew all I had to do, though, was to bide my time; eventually he would have to leave me unattended. I waited patiently until the women of the house left for the wedding and then announced to Sunil that I was turning in for the night.

Immediately I went to the bathroom and showered as fast as I could. I had intended to shave as well because I hadn't done so since arriving in Colombo, but my hands were shaking so badly I decided against it. I got out of the shower and sat on the toilet and pissed like a girl. When I stood up, a thimbleful of urine dribbled down my leg and onto the floor. I didn't have time to deal with the mess, so I just left it there.

I put on the clothes Lalanthi had picked up from Mr. Amerasinghe's and stood in front of the dressing-table mirror in my room. They were a perfect fit. Too thin or not, I looked dressed to kill.

I was sweating even before I left the house. And then jogging to Nawala Road to hail a trishaw only made it worse. By the time I got to the top of the road, gasping for breath, I felt like I needed to shower again.

A trishaw was dropping someone off on the street corner. I signaled to the driver, who pulled up alongside me. I ducked my head and squeezed into the doorless backseat. "To Ci-ci-cinnamon Grand," I stuttered.

The trishaw weaved in and out of traffic maniacally. It made me nauseous, as did the diesel exhaust. All the way to Galle Road, I covered my mouth and nose with a hand. If I hadn't been so keen to get to Anjali's wedding, I would have told the driver to turn back.

On Galle Road, a strong breeze cleared the air. The fresh, tangy smell of ocean replaced the rank odor of gasoline and garbage. In the sky seagulls swooped and cried against the setting sun. The whole world stretched out before me, like the vastness of the sea. I could feel the very essence of life pulsing through my veins. Everything would be fine, I thought. More, everything *was* fine. I could do anything. I could be anyone.

Presently we arrived at the front entrance of Cinnamon Grand. I stepped awkwardly from the trishaw, hitting my head on the frame. I laughed and shook the driver's hand. "I think I've found form and land," I said, still laughing. Then I gave him the entirety of the contents of my pockets.

He said something in Tamil I didn't understand.

In the hotel lobby, a concierge asked me if I was with the wedding party, and I said yes, yes I was. "I'm a little late, though," I apologized.

"No worries, sir," she said. "I'll take you the back way so as not to disturb anything."

She led me down a long corridor that dead-ended at a service door. "This is it," she said, opening the door. "I hope you enjoy yourself."

"I have no doubt that I will."

The wedding ceremony was already underway. All eyes were on the Kandyan dancers who were just finishing their routine. I found an empty seat at a back table. The other people at the table smiled at me as I sat down, but no one else in the ballroom appeared to have noticed me. I scanned the room for Sarasi and Nalika and Lalanthi. They were at a front table with their backs to me.

Between the *poruwa* and a large candelabrum stood the bride and groom: Anjali in a white sari, Jack in a tux. Anjali looked happy on Jack's arm, oblivious that her wedding was a sham, that Jack, *her* Jack, was a betrayer and a fraud.

Jack. A man of many faces. Which face would he assume today? Would he be a jack of spades, a knave? A jackanapes? Jack the Ripper? The Jack of Jack and Jill? A jack of all trades? Jack and the beanstalk? Jackass? Jack in the box? Jack in that little ditty 'bout Jack & Diane? The Jack who jumped over a candlestick? Or would he just be plain old Jack? Plain old fucking Jack. Fuck Jack.

I could feel saliva pooling in my mouth. I moved purposefully toward the happy couple.

They were on the *poruwa* now. The chanting had begun. When Jack saw me standing in front of him, he turned pale, as if he had seen a ghost. There was no light in his eyes. His face pixelated, momentarily became the visage of the gray-haired man.

I let the loogie fly. It hit Jack on the side of the head, marring his beautiful golden crown. "Remember me?" I said through gritted teeth.

There was a commotion behind me. I turned to see Sarasi looking at me pleadingly. Her anger and fright and mortification made her all the more striking in her lime-green dress. I watched several men from various tables descend on me as if in a dream. "Go away!" I yelled, flailing my arms frantically. But they didn't go away. A host of hands pressed in all around. Then the world went black.

About the Author

Jason Zeitler is the author of the novel *The Half-Caste*. His stories and essays have appeared in the *Journal of Experimental Fiction*, *Midwestern Gothic*, *Two Thirds North*, and elsewhere. He lives in Tucson with his wife and son. *The Breatharian and Other Stories* is his first story collection.

If you enjoyed reading *The Breatharian and Other Stories*, you might also enjoy the author's novel *The Half-Caste*, which is available at online retailers and local bookstores.